A PUFFIN BOOK

PROPERTY OF

_____

_____

LADY MARY KATHARINE PAKENHAM was born in London in 1907, the fourth of six children. She was educated mainly at home by governesses. When she grew up she became a writer and journalist, and in 1932 published her first book for adults called *In England Now* under the pen-name of Hans Duffy.

She was married in 1939 to Meysey Clive, an army officer, and they had two children. Sadly her husband was killed in action during the Second World War.

Mary wrote several novels, biographies and autobiographies, drawing on her own childhood experiences for her children's book, *Christmas with the Savages*, which was first published in 1955.

She died in Herefordshire in March 2010 at the age of 102.

MARY CLIVE

CHRISTMAS

WITH THE

SAVAGES

Illustrated by Philip Gough

A PUFFIN BOOK

PUFFIN BOOKS

UK | USA | Canada | Ireland | Australia
India | New Zealand | South Africa

Puffin Books is part of the Penguin Random House group of companies
whose addresses can be found at global.penguinrandomhouse.com.

puffinbooks.com

Penguin
Random House
UK

First published in Great Britain by Macmillan London Limited 1955
Published in Jane Nissen Books 2008
Reissued in this edition 2015

002

Text copyright © Mary Clive, 1955
Every effort has been made to trace the owner of the rights for the
artwork by Philip Gough but this has proved impossible. The publisher
would be very glad to hear from the copyright holder.

The moral right of the author and illustrator has been asserted

Set in 12.5/16.5 pt Sabon LT Std
Typeset by Jouve (UK), Milton Keynes
Printed in Great Britain by Clays Ltd, St Ives plc

A CIP catalogue record for this book is available from the British Library

ISBN: 978-0-141-36112-3

www.greenpenguin.co.uk

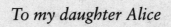

To my daughter Alice

Contents

1. My Own Home

WHEN I was a little girl I lived in a tall London house which you would have thought rather grand and very dull. You might also have thought that my parents were dreadfully old and stiff, but I was used to them; and anyway grown-up people did not scamper about in the way that they do now.

I was an only child and I was allowed to come into the drawing room a good deal. I believe visitors thought me spoilt and a bore, but I loved getting away from the quiet of the schoolroom to the rustle and chatter of callers. It was a treat to come downstairs, even if I was made to stay behind the velvet curtains which separated the dull back drawing room from the pretty front room. I was quite happy sitting there holding a book which I had read over twenty times, looking out on the chimney-pots of the mews (no two were alike and some of them turned in the wind) and enjoying the murmur of voices. Every now and then there would be bursts of idiotic laughter. I had often listened to grown-up jokes and I did not think them funny, but I looked forward to the time when I should be the first to laugh, instead of coming in at the end with a ha! ha! ha! which was loud but not very natural. Indeed, I longed and longed to be grown-up, and sometimes I used to clutch my skirts when crossing the road and pretend that that happy time had already come. How elegantly I meant to hold my starer-spectacles to my eyes! How graciously would I say 'charming' and 'delightful'! And how mysteriously my mauve dresses would rustle along the passage!

Mine was an uneventful life, and when my parents went on visits, as they often did, it was duller still. There was nothing to make one day different from another – just dressing and going to bed, meals and lessons and walks in the park. My governess was not unkind, but she was old and sad and wrapped up in her own thoughts, and I got away from her whenever I could.

But occasionally things happened even to me, and one day, when I was about eight, I remember my lessons being interrupted by something a little unusual. My father and mother had been away on a visit to Scotland and I was very much looking forward to their coming back – in fact, although I was supposed to be learning dates, I was really pretending that I was in the drawing room talking to visitors. I had just opened my mouth to yawn and my governess had just opened hers to tell me to pay attention, when there was a knock on the door and Frederick the footman came in with a telegram.

In those days telegrams were not sent over the telephone. A special telegraph boy brought them to the house and the butler carried them into the drawing room on a little silver tray. Their envelopes were a sort of dirty orange colour, quite unlike anything else, and when one came I was always dreadfully curious and wanted to know what was in it, but I was hardly ever told.

On this occasion, as the telegram was addressed to my governess, it was laid on a common wooden tray. She took it with the tips of her fingers and I could see that she was nervous, but as I had been told never to look at a person reading a telegram for fear it was Bad News, I turned away my eyes and stared at the buttons on Frederick's uniform – no, I'm afraid he wasn't a powdered footman, but he wore a nice brown coat with brass buttons and green trousers. The buttons were heaving slightly as he was out of breath, having run all the way up from the basement. (There were flights and flights of stairs before you reached the schoolroom landing which was fenced in with wire netting so that I should not fall over the banisters.) At the same time as I watched the buttons I was on the alert, waiting for my governess to faint. If she had done so I meant to dash into my bedroom and fetch the water jug. I was thinking what a lovely splash it would make if I emptied it over her, when she spoke. Her voice was solemn but quite calm.

'Well, Evelyn, this is from your mother. She says your father has fallen ill and has gone into a nursing home in Edinburgh. So they have had to postpone their return. Frederick, will you tell them downstairs that they have had to postpone their return.'

Frederick said, 'Oh, they know that already. Mr Benson had a telegram too.'

My governess got pink. She never really was asked to pass on messages to Mr Benson who thought himself much more important than she was.

'Thank you, Frederick,' she said, 'now we must go on with our lessons.'

I gloomily wondered how long it would be before I was allowed down into the drawing room again.

'What's father got?' I asked.

'Something internal,' said my governess. I knew better than to ask anything more.

After that, letters came from my mother, some of them addressed to me. I could not read her writing, and when they were read aloud to me I didn't always listen. One day, when my governess was reading one of these letters, she stopped and said:

'That *will* be exciting for you.'

My mind was far away, thinking of the dress in which I meant to be presented at court.

'What will?' I asked, coming back with a jerk.

'Why, I've just read it to you. Your mother says that as she won't be back for Christmas she has arranged for you to spend it with Lady Tamerlane.'

'Old Lady Tamerlane! Me and old Lady Tamerlane spend Christmas together!'

Lady Tamerlane often came to see my mother and I knew quite well what she looked like. Although she was old she was brisk, and although she was not playful she sometimes gave me half-crowns. She and my mother used to do acrostics and read Italian poetry together, and I had been told that she was very clever. I did not really believe this as I had heard her make mistakes about quite ordinary things like fire engines and the zoo, and when she came to call, the bursts of grown-up laughter always seemed particularly silly. I tried to imagine what Christmas with Lady Tamerlane would be like.

'I think I might manage the acrostics if she showed me how to do them,' I said at length, 'but I don't think I could bear the Italian poetry.'

'I don't suppose you'll have to,' said my governess. 'There'll be lots of grown-up people to amuse Lady Tamerlane. All you will have to do is to play with her grandchildren. She has a lot of grandchildren – I don't quite know how many; but there will be the little Savages anyway.'

'Little savages? Will they be cannibals?'

'No, of course not. "Savage" is just their name. They're ordinary children, and very nice children too, I expect. It will be fun for you having Christmas with the Savages.'

'How do you know they are nice?'

'Lady Tamerlane's grandchildren are sure to be nice,' replied my governess.

I rearranged my ideas. Instead of just me and Lady Tamerlane there would be a huge crowd.

'Will it be a house party?' I had heard of 'house parties' and I could imagine people sitting about in trailing clothes and elegant attitudes like the pictures in the fashion magazines. I could also imagine that in the middle of them would be myself playing the harp. I meant to have a gold harp painted with green trees like one I had seen in a shop, and an ivory one for best. Except that there were no wings or clouds, my idea of a house party was much the same as my idea of heaven.

'Well,' said my governess, 'yes, I suppose you might call it a sort of house party.'

'Then I shall be very pleased to accept Lady Tamerlane's kind invitation,' I said.

2. The Journey Down

MY GOVERNESS of course had holidays at Christmas, and so I set off for the house party with Marguerite, my Swiss nursery maid. Marguerite was supposed to speak French to me but she was a poor, frightened creature whom I treated like mud, and who hardly spoke to anybody in any language.

We had lunch at half past twelve, and the food was rather different from what we generally had – there was fish instead of meat, and cake instead of pudding. I don't quite know what was the point of this, but it helped me to feel excited and rather sick. Then our luggage was carried down. I had an immense trunk with a rounded top and straps, and Marguerite had a brown tin box tied up with cords.

I was allowed to blow the whistle for the taxi. The whistle hung in the hall and one blew and blew until a taxi came up. It was a very noisy proceeding, but everyone did it.

Frederick went with us to the station to see us on to the train. I hardly recognized him in his outdoor clothes, but they seemed to make him very frisky, for he joked the whole way. I laughed like anything, and even Marguerite smiled occasionally.

Paddington was our station, and as far as I can remember, it looked very much as it does today. In fact the 1.45, which we caught, is still running, although I suppose the engine is a different shape and the carriages are not decorated with so many squiggles.

Frederick found us a porter and bought us tickets, and then led us along the platform to a group of children whom he had at once recognized as the little Savages. How he knew them by sight I can't think, but Frederick was very clever at that sort of thing.

I looked eagerly at the house party. There were two boys, two girls, two nursery maids (in little bonnets trimmed with black velvet), a baby, a nurse and a man who was obviously their footman. They all looked rather fussed – even the baby had a worried frown – and when Frederick introduced us, the only thing the nurse said was:

'Oh well, they must go in another carriage. There's no room here.' She then asked the porter which way the train went.

There was a howl from her children. '*Really*, Nana. Can't you *see*!'

'It's just as well to be quite sure,' said their nurse. The children stared at me and I stared back at them, and then Marguerite and I got into an empty first class carriage – I always travelled first class for fear of catching something. Frederick went off to watch our luggage being put into the van and came back with *Tit-Bits*, a paper which my mother always bought for me on journeys. I sat down pretending I was reading it while Frederick stayed at the window to encourage Marguerite with jokes, but soon two of the Savage children came down the corridor and stared in at me, pressing their noses against the glass until the tips went white. They whispered to each other and looked at me and whispered to each other again, and then they opened the door and the girl said very severely:

'Are you a Cavalier or a Roundhead?'

I did History every day with my governess and if they had asked me about Egbert, Aethelbert or

Aethelred I should have known what to answer.
But my history book was so long that I had only
got a quarter of the way through it, and I knew
nothing about the wars of Charles I. It was like
being asked 'oranges or lemons?', only worse. I
looked at their faces but could learn nothing from
them, so I gave up trying to guess right and, being
anxious to please, said:

'Which ought I to be?'

'You ought to be a Roundhead,' said the boy,
scowling at me.

'No, you didn't. You ought to be a Cavalier,'
said the girl.

'Can't I be both?'

The girl snorted with contempt. 'You're as bad
as Minnie,' she said. 'When she was new I asked
her to be a Cavalier and she said she would,
only she'd just promised Master Harry to be a
Roundhead and she didn't know what either of
them were. And she's only just left school!'

I saw that I had made an awful blunder and to
change the subject I asked them their names.

'We are the young Savages,' said the boy. 'Harry
is me, and Rosamund is her. Rosamund is the
former girl and Betty is the latter girl.' This
seemed to be a family joke and they both laughed.

'I am Evelyn,' I said.

'That's not a girl's name,' said Rosamund.

'Yes, it is. It's mine. And what's more it's always been mine. I was christened it.'

'You can't have been,' said Rosamund. 'I expect it's only a nickname.'

'When girls start using boys' names,' said Harry, looking at me sternly, 'the worst may happen.'

There was an awkward silence. I found the Savages very difficult to talk to. I was, you remember, an only child and I did not see many other children, but the few I had played with had been much more friendly than these two. I did so want the Savages to like me and everything I said seemed to be wrong. I was glad when the train started.

'Come into our carriage,' said Rosamund.

Without a word to poor Marguerite I followed her into the next compartment which was already very crowded, not so much by people as by handbags and baskets which had been unpacked all over it.

The nurse sat by the window with the baby on her knee. She kept her hand over her face as though the children were more than she could bear, but the baby, wrapped in shawls and a red-riding-hood cloak, watched everything with its big brown eyes. The eldest boy, Lionel, had his head bent low over a book. I had noticed him on the platform and had decided that he should be my special friend, but he did not look up when I came into the carriage. The book he was reading had nice big print and coloured pictures, but I was sorry to see that it was called *The Story of Greece*.

The other child, Betty, was a fat little thing with very red cheeks and very white hair. She also had a book, a picture book which turned out to be a history of England written in rhyme. Betty could not really read, but she recited over and over again in a maddening sing-song:

> '*He fell into the* power
> *Of Leopold Duke of Austria,*
> *Who shut him up in a* tower.'

'What a hopeless family!' I thought. 'How can one make friends with any of them? Even Lady Tamerlane and her Italian poetry would be better than this. At least she did call one "dear child" and gave one half-crowns.'

'Minnie and May have gone third class,' said Harry. 'I'm glad we don't have to go third class.

Dada says when the train breaks down, first class passengers stay where they are, second class passengers get out and walk, third class passengers get out and push. Will Minnie and May have to push us if the train breaks down?'

'Of course they will if Dada says so,' said Rosamund. She could not resist adding, 'And I expect they will make *you* push too.'

'They won't,' said Harry.

'They will!' said Rosamund, who was a terrible tease.

'Won't,' shouted Harry, and catching Rosamund by the hair, he pulled her head down to the floor.

'Will,' screamed Rosamund, almost upside down, and her face scarlet.

I expected the nurse to interfere, but she took no notice. The baby, however, broke into a delighted chuckle. I felt I ought to help Rosamund and was looking at Harry's sailor suit, wondering which bit of it I should grab, when a piercing scream from Betty made us all look round. She had been fidgeting with the window and had dropped her history book down the slit where the glass goes. Rosamund and Harry forgot their quarrel and rushed to help her. 'My corns,' said their nurse mildly but without taking her hand from her eyes, as they stumbled over her feet.

'I expect it's gone on to the line,' said Harry.

'No, it will be still in the door,' said Rosamund.

They pulled the window up and down twenty times, but the only result was that the carriage became very cold. (It was, of course, December.) Betty looked so miserable that I felt rather motherly towards her. I took her back to my carriage and read *Tit-Bits* to her for a time, but as it was really a grown-up's paper with long words in it, she soon stopped listening.

I had been taught to sit still in a railway train and to bear the boredom in silence, but Betty had not.

'Look at the telegraph wires, Betty,' I said. 'Isn't it funny the way they seem to go up and down and cross over each other?'

'I 'ates telegraph wires,' said Betty. 'Aren't we nearly there? How much longer? What time is it now?'

She fidgeted so much I sent her back to her own carriage and sat alone with Marguerite. I felt annoyed with the Savages for being so difficult to talk to, and the journey seemed endless. Every now and then Rosamund and Harry looked in with a bit of news such as 'The Roundheads have utterly crushed the Cavaliers, but the Cavaliers are going to rout them tomorrow' or 'Betty's been sick'. After passing Reading they sang 'You can't buy pyjamas at Huntley & Palmers' for quite ten minutes. Whenever I saw them coming I tried to look haughty, crossing one leg over the other and holding *Tit-Bits* up to my face. I admired the grown-up way that Lionel sat in his corner reading, and I hoped that he somehow knew that I was doing it too.

However, even the longest journey ends some time, and it was not even dark when we bundled out at a station. There seemed to be a lot of us when we all were standing together on the platform watching the trunks being pulled out of the van – and you never saw so much luggage as those Savages had brought. Regardless of the other people, they broke out into a chant. Chanting was, I discovered later, a habit of theirs, although they none of them had the faintest idea of tune. The words went:

> 'Brown paper parcels,
> Only just a few,
> The perambulator and the bath
> And the dear old cockatoo.'

'If only we had a *man*,' said the nurse feebly, and as she spoke the stationmaster appeared and rallied the whole mob of us and marched us outside through a special gate. I was hustled with the nurse and baby and Betty into a brougham, which is a small cab lined with dark-blue cloth and having a peculiar fusty smell. The rest went in a larger carriage known as the station bus. Betty was insulted at being shoved in with the baby and made a great to-do, and indeed it was clear that the other children with the nursery maids were going to have much more fun than we were: but the stationmaster slammed the door and off we drove.

Betty at once began to sing a chant which went:

> *'He snapped a faggot-band,*
> *He plied his work and Lucy took*
> *The lantern in her hand.'*

After she had sung it six times over I asked her who 'he' was and what was a 'faggot-band'. Betty replied at once that 'he' was a cat and so was Lucy, and 'snapped a faggot-band' was the sort of unexpected pounce that cats sometimes make. I said Lucy couldn't be a cat as cats couldn't carry lanterns, but she said that her cats always carried lanterns. I asked her to stop singing anyway as it was annoying.

'It's nothing to do with me. I don't even like it,' replied Betty and went on singing. Presently she changed to a song of her own called 'The Seam and the Sycamore'. The Seam, she explained, were millions of horrid little white caterpillars who live underground and go about with lanterns (like cats) while the Sycamore was a very nice cow. 'They keep trying to catch him. Sometimes they do but he always escapes in the end.'

And she started off:

> 'So *they went along along,*
> *So they went abing abong.*'

It was all like that. I raised my eyebrows and looked at the nurse, hoping that she would stop Betty, but she didn't seem to notice anything.

At last we got there.

By this time it was very nearly dark, but peering out of the window I was able to make out cedar trees and a house that was very big and very plain, except for the front door which was guarded by great pillars.

The brougham stopped, however, at a quite ordinary door at the side. My dignity was hurt and I was further annoyed to find that Lady Tamerlane was not there to say how-do-you-do. Instead we were welcomed by Mr O'Sullivan the butler, and Mrs Peabody the housekeeper, and when the other children had pushed past them and gone thundering off up the wooden stairs to the nursery, I thought I would say something grand to make them see that I was different from the ordinary child.

Noticing a gas bracket which Mr O'Sullivan was lighting by banging with a pole, I said:

'Don't you have electric light here?'

Instead of being impressed with my knowledge of the world Mrs Peabody merely thought that I was finding fault with her precious house.

'Why, you *are* a little Londoner,' she quickly replied. 'You must remember that you are in the country now.'

'Some houses in the country do have electric light,' I said, thinking that Mrs Peabody did not know this interesting fact and would be grateful for the information. 'I've stayed in one that has.'

Mrs Peabody was not a bit grateful.

'Candles is better for you,' she said, as she started upstairs. She was one of those grown-ups who think that children hear nothing unless you are actually talking to them, so she added in her ordinary voice to the nurse, 'What an interfering little madam she is.'

We turned into the nursery passage where children were running in and out of rooms and shouting to each other. I put my hands to my ears.

'What an abominable noise,' I said, making one last effort to impress Mrs Peabody. 'It gives me a headache.'

'Little girls don't have headaches,' swiftly retorted Mrs Peabody, and I decided she was too stupid to bother with any longer.

My room was interesting. It had a Kate Greenaway wallpaper, and great grey pictures of stags, and above the mantelpiece a picture of a lady in evening dress leading a little boy in yellow underclothes over some stepping stones. *Crossing the Brook* it was called. Mrs Peabody saw me looking at it and said:

'Her Ladyship says that picture is very valuable and oughtn't to be here.'

It made me feel important but slightly worried to find myself the guardian of treasure. Suppose a burglar should come!

'And are those valuable, too?' I asked, pointing to the stags.

Mrs Peabody didn't really know. 'They're all of Scotland,' she said brightly, 'and exactly like it, too.'

I thought it looked a horrible place, mist and mountains and wild animals, and I wondered why my parents should trouble to go there. It would not suit their usual habits. In my mind I could see my father trotting off to his club with his top hat and umbrella, and my mother going out calling with her veils and flounces and her silver card-case, and I could not imagine what either of them would do if left alone on a mountain with nothing but stags. It seemed so sad – almost as sad as me being left alone among the Savages. I felt very sorry for myself and homesick for that nice London drawing room, where everything I did and said was admired as a matter of course.

3. The First Evening

I HAD set out with the idea of getting to know all the Tamerlane Hall house party, but it was such a large one that I was a long time making out who belonged to whom; in fact I never did really discover how many grown-ups there were downstairs.

To begin with, there were three sets of children, grandchildren of old Lady Tamerlane, and they all had nurses and nursery maids as well as mothers and fathers. The nurses were all called Mrs This and Mrs That although they weren't married, but I will call them Nana Savage and so on, as it is easier to remember.

The extraordinary Savages I had already sorted in my mind, and I was even able to tell which of the nursery maids was Minnie and which May. Then there were the Glens with a fierce little nurse who made sarcastic remarks, though the Glens themselves were gentle, attractive children. Peggy had long hair that she could sit on, and Peter looked simply sweet like the little boy in the picture called *Bubbles*. I had high hopes of making friends with them. There were also two older Glens called Malcolm and Alister, but they were big boys who lived downstairs with the grown-ups.

The third set of children were unkindly nicknamed the Howliboos. They were quite small, pretty little things but nervous, specially Tommy, the eldest.

Later I came to realize that Nana Howliboo thought she ought to be top Nana because Father Howliboo was the most important of the fathers; but Nana Glen and Nana Savage had been coming to Tamerlane much longer than she had, and they did not agree with her. I don't think Nana Savage bothered much about it, but Nana Glen had been pouring out in that nursery ever since Malcolm was a baby and she did not mean to take a back seat.

The nursery was not a particularly big room, and when I first sidled in, it seemed very full and very noisy. I stood unhappily by myself, watching tea being laid and wondering if I should ever get used to the hubbub. Before we had settled down to it we heard a brisk step in the passage and Lady Tamerlane was among us.

There was at once a shout of 'Grandmama!' and Baby Savage hammered on the table with a spoon.

Lady Tamerlane briskly kissed us all on both cheeks, one after the other. When it came to my turn I made a little speech.

'It is very kind of you to ask me to your house party, Lady Tamerlane.'

'Well, dear child, I hope you will enjoy it,' replied she. 'Your name is Everline, ain't it?'

'No, it's Evelyn, after my Great-Aunt Evelyn,' I was beginning to explain, but Lady Tamerlane was already kissing the next child.

'Well, run along, Everline, and have a good tea. You'll come down to the library afterwards.' She did not listen to one, but her bright eyes were darting round the room and she spotted Marguerite. She asked her in French if she were comfortable. Marguerite was too overcome to answer, but she curtseyed low.

Then in stumped Betty, saying:

'What I've come for is tea and praise.'

'Praise? Whatever for?' said her grandmother, attempting to kiss her.

'For everything I've done today,' said Betty, dodging the kiss and going to the table to see what sort of cake there was.

Lady Tamerlane whisked away as quickly as she had come, and I asked at once:

'When can I go to the library? Now?'

'Six o'clock, when they all go down,' said Nana Glen snubbingly.

I was disappointed as I had expected to have the grown-ups to myself, but I still hoped that with my pretty manners I should be able to outshine the other children.

At tea, all the babies sat at a round table in the middle of the room, while Nana Glen poured out for us big ones at a long table at the side. She helped the Glen children first with the firmness with which she did everything, but after that she was fair enough.

Finding myself next to Lionel I began a grown-up conversation.

'I have a delightful bedroom,' I said. 'It has pictures of deer.'

'Stags you mean,' said Lionel. 'That's the stink room. She's got the stink room, the stink room, the stink room.'

Lionel seemed very difficult to talk to and not as grown-up as he looked, but I tried again.

'Have all the rooms got names?'

'Rather. There's the Pigsty, the Dungeon, Blue Ruin, Hades and the Unbreathy-air Hole.'

'They're not very pretty names.'

'Who wants pretty names? Heave over the jam.'

I thought I might make myself useful passing things, so I asked Nana Glen if she would like some butter. She had the teapot in one hand and the hot-water jug in the other and said:

'Save your breath to cool your porridge.'

I had never heard this expression before, and every time one of the nursery maids was sent to fetch something (and they were springing up from their chairs the whole time) I expected to see them return with a bowl of porridge. However, everyone had finished and had rushed away from the table while I was still eating bread and butter.

'Good gracious, what a slow eater the child is,' said Nana Glen. 'You'll be still sitting there looking at your plate when the others have gone downstairs.'

This was a dreadful idea, and I gulped down what was left and hurried off to get dressed.

And what a performance that was! But as it happened every day we were all used to it. By the mysterious light of a couple of candles I put on clean frilly knickers, a clean frilly petticoat and clean socks. My shoes were of a purplish colour called bronze. My frock was very elaborate. It was trimmed with a coarse sort of lace called Irish crochet, and it had white ribbon threaded through it in several places. All the time that poor Marguerite was trying to dress me I kept darting away to look at things, and she had to follow me about making little bleating noises. I jumped on to the armchair and the bed, and was as tiresome as I could be, but in the end I stood still for her to brush my hair for, after all, I did want to look my best when I went downstairs.

I could hear noises that suggested that in other rooms other children were being equally tiresome, but at six o'clock out we all came on to the landing, looking as good as angels. All the girls were in white. Their dresses were hideously over-decorated according to modern ideas, but Rosamund and Betty wore wide pink sashes which must really have been quite pretty. The beauty of the party, however, was undoubtedly Peter, who wore a black velvet suit with a lace collar and a crimson sash.

The youngest Howliboo and the Savage baby were left behind, but the two eldest Howliboos were there, dragged along by their Nana.

With a yell the six big children raced off down the passage and round the corner. I took Tommy Howliboo's hand. He was a nice little boy and we were glad of each other's company, though I couldn't help wishing that he would come along a bit faster as I didn't want to miss any fun that was going on in the library.

We went down the front stairs, which were very grand. On the walls were Chinese hangings, red silk embroidered with dragons.

'Dwagon 'tairs,' said Tommy, pointing them out to me.

'Oh, Tommy, it's rude to point,' said his Nana, who was very refined.

'All dat wed is blood,' went on Tommy, licking his lips. 'At night, dwagons tum down and go pat, pat, pat wound de 'ouse. I wun too kick for 'em, but dey cot Betty an' tore 'er fwock.'

Having thoroughly frightened himself he then said he couldn't possibly walk any farther, and his Nana had to carry him while I dragged down the little girl.

Outside the library door we found the other children waiting for us. Lionel was passing the time by teasing Peter, calling him Pumpkin Eater – an insult which made Peter blind with fury. Lionel had taken up a strong position behind a china cabinet, but at one moment it seemed as if even that would not protect him against Peter's charge. However, Peter had just enough self-control left to avoid the cabinet and merely crashed into the gong.

The terrific boom made us all jump, and both the Howliboos began to howl.

Peggy said '*Really*, Peter,' and Rosamund said '*Honestly*, Lionel,' in very superior voices. The library door was opened from the inside, and we all swarmed out of the gloom of the hall into the heavenly splendour of the library.

It was a long room, so long, in fact, that one could hardly see the other end of it. About halfway down was a fireplace round which a lot of grown-ups were sitting. They were mostly women, as the men of the party made a point of avoiding the library between six and seven. I found out afterwards that they shut themselves up in a room into which women and children were never allowed to go, though I once peeped in through the hinge of the door. It smelt of cigars, and all round the walls were very unlifelike pictures of racehorses.

As soon as they were inside the library, the Savages made a rush at the various tables of bagatelle and other games that were dotted about it. At once there was a noise of balls banging and shouts of 'My turn,' 'Rotten shot,' and so on. There was one very fascinating game which I have never seen anywhere else. Imagine a table with little pillars and arches and balustrades fitted on to it, and among them a lot of ninepins. You spun a powerful top among them, and it went through the arches and knocked down the ninepins. Somebody or other always seemed to be playing it, so whenever I think of that big grand room, I always hear the whizz of tops and the clatter-clatter of ninepins.

I myself was not used to playing games of any sort. Besides, I had my own plans. Pretending to look at this and that, I worked my way quietly down the room till I had got to the grown-up district. There the first person to take any notice of me was a dim middle-aged lady who asked me to hold her wool, but as soon as she had tied me to herself I began to think that anyone else in the room would have been more amusing, and I kept letting the skein fall off my fingers. I entirely forgot the pretty manners of which I was so proud, and instead of answering her questions I tried to listen to everybody else's conversation.

I was particularly attracted by the two elder Glen boys who were playing chess close at hand, and I screwed round my head to watch them. I thought I understood how the game went, and when one of the boys hesitated for a very long time I could not resist butting in.

'I should move that big one,' I said.

Both the boys looked up and stared at me as though I were some peculiar sort of animal. I smiled as nicely as I knew how and dropped the skein of wool for the tenth time.

'Oh, you would, would you?' said one of the boys in biting tones, and down went their heads again.

I hoped that nobody had heard me getting this terrible snub, but fortunately Rosamund was going round the circle asking everybody if they were Cavalier or Roundhead, and writing the answer down in a notebook.

'Which are you?' someone asked her.

'Cavalier, of course,' said Rosamund. 'I'm Rupert of the Rhine. Naturally.'

'Are you all equally keen on history?' somebody else asked.

'Betty is,' said Harry. He took a sort of fatherly pride in Betty and liked to make her show off her tricks. 'Tell them about history, Betty.'

Betty was apt to be either very bold or very shy. On this occasion she was very bold. She planted herself on the hearthrug with her legs apart.

'My one is Leopold, Duke of Austria. I am going to marry him.'

'But what about him shutting up poor Richard in a dungeon?' said one of the aunts. Everyone at Tamerlane Hall knew a lot about history. 'Stone cold and pitch dark, I expect.'

'No, it weren't,' contradicted Betty. 'It were stone hot and pitch light. And I shall also marry Lars Porsena. And Guy Fawkes, too. He used his fireworks to blow up the House of the Parlourmaid.'

'Can you tell us about the Whigs and Tories?' asked another Aunt.

'Aunt Hester,' answered Betty, 'I know about only two sort of wigs. Hair wigs and earwigs.'

I thought this was enough about history, so I dropped the wool altogether and joined Betty on the hearthrug and told them that I had started French. This had the effect I wanted, and everyone turned and looked at me.

'Do you do "French without Tears"?' said an aunt. 'Let me see, how does it begin? About Robert and Charles, isn't it? *Robert est grand et Charles est petit*. Who knows what that means?'

Perhaps her accent was rather more Frenchified than the accents we were used to. At any rate no one seemed anxious to speak, and the aunt repeated it over again very slowly. '*Robert est grand*' (here she put her hand high in the air) '*et Charles est petit*.' Here she put it very low.

'Oh, I see now,' said Harry. 'Robert is in an aeroplane.'

'And Charles is a cat,' chipped in Betty.

There was a burst of foolish grown-up laughter, and to change the subject I pointed to a large oil painting and asked what it was meant to be of. It was indeed a very strange picture. In the middle was a boy, or possibly a girl, dressed in armour and holding a sword in an affected sort of way. At the side a lady with powdered hair was running in and holding up her hands, also in an affected sort of way. Down at one corner crouched a mischievous-looking boy (or girl perhaps), and down at the other corner was a dead monster.

'Why, that's St George and the Dragon,' said Lady Tamerlane. 'I expect you all know the story.'

None of us could honestly say that we did.

'How very shocking,' said Lady Tamerlane, laughing. 'Well, I must tell it to you.'

'That will be delightful,' I said. Rosamund kicked me. The Savages not only did not make pretty speeches themselves, they could not bear people who did. All the children gathered round except the Howliboos, who had been removed long ago, and Lionel, who went on playing tops by himself, bang – bang, clatter – clatter.

'Well, once upon a time,' began Lady Tamerlane in the special voice that she always put on when she was going to tell a story, 'the kingdom of Silene was devastated by a terrible dragon.'

'That's not true!' shouted Betty. She was standing full in front of her grandmother and the old lady blinked but went on.

'Beautiful maidens had to be sacrificed to this monster. They were chosen by lot and then taken out into the wilderness where the dragon –'

'That's not true!' shouted Betty again. The trouble with Betty was that ever since she had made Lionel cry by telling him that mermaids were 'only pretend' she had set up as the family debunker.

She wanted everyone to know that she was too clever to believe in fairies or magic, and she took the whole St George story to be a roundabout way of treating her like a baby. Perhaps it should also be mentioned that though Betty scorned fairies she was very frightened of witches, specially after dark, and if it came to dragons, no one scuttled faster past the Chinese hangings on the front stairs.

'One day the lot fell upon the king's own daughter, and with weeping and wailing she was led out into the wilderness to await the dragon.'

'Not true!' shouted Betty again, this time simply yelling and going purple in the face with the effort. As her grandmother had taken no notice of her other interruptions she imagined they had not been heard.

Lady Tamerlane looked round to see if Betty's mother was there, but as she wasn't she went on again, though slightly louder and faster.

'Now it chanced that a knight called George was riding by, and hearing that a terrible dragon –'

'Look who's come,' said Rosamund. We all turned round and saw with relief the silent figure of Minnie standing in the door, ready to take her. victim to bed. Betty recognized her doom and went obediently but with her hands over her ears and muttering 'Not true, not true,' till out of hearing and probably the whole way up to the nursery as well.

Lady Tamerlane finished her story in peace and we played Snakes and Ladders, and at intervals silent nursery maids appeared and removed both Harry and Peter. As the children thinned out the grown-ups seemed easier to get at, but just as I was about to make advances to the youngest and prettiest aunt, who I felt sure would appreciate me, we three girls, Peggy, Rosamund and myself, were told to run on up to bed.

We all linked arms and as soon as we got outside the door Rosamund said, 'Listen, I have an idea. Don't let's go straight to bed. Instead, let's run round the house.'

Peggy and I agreed at once, and with whispering and giggling we turned our backs on the dragon stairs and tiptoed through the shadows to the outer hall.

Here there was a strong smell of cigars and the murmur of gruff voices. Two of the uncles, knowing that the children's hour was nearly over, had come out of their lair in the smoking room but had apparently not made up their minds where to go next. Once of them was in a leather armchair with a hood over it, rather like a sitting-down sentry box; the other had his back to us and we could only see the top of his bald head.

'Let's go and smack Uncle Algy on his bald head,' suggested Rosamund.

'Dare we?' I asked.

'Oh yes. Nobody minds Uncle Algy.'

We crept forward on our hands and knees, quiet as mice, or so we imagined; but mice really are not a bit quiet and our frocks rustled and crackled. The uncles went on talking, however, and we crawled closer and closer, until Rosamund the bold actually reared up with lifted hand ready for a smashing blow. At that moment the bald head reared up also and a face looked over the back of the chair, and the horrified Rosamund beheld, not the harmless, smiling wrinkles of her Great-Uncle Algy, but fierce moustaches and bulging eyes. 'Aunt Muriel's Husband!' cried Rosamund.

'Shoo!' he cried, waving his newspaper above his head.

We sprang to our feet with a rending noise as Peggy trod on the flounce of her frock, and we dashed out of the hall and down a long passage. The passage was dark, being lit by only one gas lamp at the far end of it, but I followed the others blindly.

'Salvation!' cried Rosamund who read a lot of books and liked long words, and swerving suddenly, plunged into the dark under a flight of stairs. Peggy and I quickly followed, diving head first over a chintz-covered ottoman that stood in front of her hiding place.

For what seemed a very long time we lay in a heap with beating hearts waiting for the avengers, but no one came.

'Who is Aunt Muriel's Husband?' I asked in a whisper.

'Oh, he's awful,' said both girls. 'Aunt Muriel married him and then she died, and now he can't be got rid of.'

'She left him behind with us like a fox leaves its scent,' said Peggy to make it clearer.

'I'll tell you something,' said Rosamund. 'Even Grandmama abhors him.'

'In that case what a pity you didn't give him a real good bash,' I said.

We giggled some more and waited some more, and then Rosamund said:

'Let's go to bed. If we creep up the blue stairs no one will see us.'

We stole cautiously out and tiptoed up the blue stairs, but at the top we suddenly felt safe and tore whooping down the long passage which led to the nursery wing. As we turned the corner whom should we see but old Lady Tamerlane going the round of the bedrooms to say goodnight. We tried to dash past her but she put out her arms and collared us.

To our amazement she did not seem to realize that we were desperadoes. She did not even seem to notice that we had been naughty. She merely kissed us and passed on.

Stunned by this escape we went in silence to our rooms.

Marguerite was waiting for me with my nightgown spread out on a chair and everything else ready for me. I was quite nice to her for a change, partly because I was too tired by the people I had met and the things I had seen to play her up, and partly because she reminded me of home. My London bedroom seemed so far away that I could hardly believe I had been in it no longer ago than that very morning.

'What I've been through today!' I said. Then my eye lit on the picture of the lady and the little boy which Mrs Peabody said was valuable. 'I hope the burglars won't come tonight – I'm simply too exhausted.' The candle was placed so that the stags were in shadow but I could see the children on the wallpaper. The same ones were repeated over and over again and they were all so alike that it was difficult to count how many were actually different. Marguerite tucked me up and I kissed her without meaning to. 'Sorry,' I said, and then, 'Oh well, it doesn't matter. You're not much good, Marguerite, but at least you do belong to me.'

One never knew how much Marguerite understood, but this was more polite than the sort of thing I usually said, and she looked surprised and pleased.

4. The Garden

SWING doors covered with green baize separated the back part of the house from the front. I never made out the full extent of the back regions with the knife rooms and lamp rooms and boot-holes and store cupboards, let alone its warren of bedrooms, but I have a distinct recollection of looking in through the kitchen door and seeing meat roasting on a spit, though what turned the spit or how I got there I can't remember. The only passage I was ever sure about was the way to Mrs Peabody's sitting room.

This was one of the cosiest rooms in the house and we loved going to it. For one thing it was next door to the still room where two still-room maids were always making cakes, and there was generally a mixing-basin to lick out. For another thing it was as full of knick-knacks as a curiosity shop.

That first morning I was taken down to it by Peggy and Peter. Rosamund and Harry had gone out riding and Lionel had slipped away to his mother. The rest of the children were getting ready to go out, a weary process in nursery days.

You would have laughed at the clothes which we wore for playing in the garden. They were last year's Sunday ones and were not at all suitable. My hat was a huge object made of velvet. The brim was lined with pleated satin and it was trimmed with a wreath of big satin roses. My coat had a floppy collar of broderie anglaise and we wore button boots which took a long time to do up and let in the water. However, we did not think that we looked funny, and as we had never heard of dungarees or wellington boots or pixie hoods, we didn't want them. We went happily down to Mrs Peabody's room and she was so kind to us that I changed my mind about her and decided that she was very nice after all.

She let us go round her room fingering everything and asking questions. Among her treasures which I can remember were a yellow china pillar as high as myself, a carved bear painting a landscape, a vase full of peacocks' feathers and a model of Tamerlane Hall made in sugar. But the thing which really caught my fancy was a small glass swan.

There was nothing very extraordinary about it, but the moment I saw it I loved it. I stroked it and held it up to the light and resolved that when I grew up I should search the world until I found one like it.

Peter was more interested in a boomerang which Mrs Peabody's brother who was dead had sent her from Australia. It was just a plain piece of wood with a bend in it, and she told us that the Australian natives threw it at animals and killed them with it. If they failed to hit the animal, the funny shape it was made it turn round and come back into their hands again.

We found this hard to believe, and Peter begged to be allowed to take it into the garden and try. Mrs Peabody did not really want to let him, as the boomerang was one of her greatest treasures, but no old lady could ever resist Peter's angelic face and beautiful curls.

'Well, all right,' she said at last, 'if you promise me to be very, very careful with it.'

We promised, and then we heard the rest of the nursery party descending upon us. Betty stumped in first, demanding Mrs Peabody's collie dog, Kim, of whom she was very fond. She put her arms round his neck and kissed him again and again. She would insist that he was the 'real Lord Tamerlane' and owned everything in the house. She had noticed that this shocked and embarrassed the nurses so she made a point of saying it, especially in front of strangers.

'Good morning, Lord Tamerlane,' she said. 'I hope you haven't been missing me. I wanted to come before but I wasn't let. Thank you for putting me in a bed instead of a cot. Tommy's got the cot now. It's a horrid one. You can't see out of it.'

I don't know how much of this Kim understood, but he certainly looked pleased to be made a fuss of, and he let Betty crawl over him while he sat with his mouth open panting hard and smiling.

Then the prams had to be got out and the four babies fitted into them. Mr O'Sullivan was flitting about – he always appeared when anything was happening. Nursery maids were sent upstairs for things that had been forgotten, and after several false starts they trundled off.

Betty went with the prams, so as to give Kim a walk. In a way these walks were painful to her, as she had an idea that the Jersey cows in the park would object to Kim being the same curious colour as themselves and suddenly rush down on him to punish him for it. As long as they were in the park she walked beside him with her hand on his collar to protect him, but it was anxious work for her.

We three big ones waved till they were out of sight and then went off to play in the garden. Marguerite was supposed to be looking after us, but she flitted round like a grey ghost and we took no notice of her whatever.

Soon we found that none of us could make the boomerang work, so we laid it on a seat and forgot about it.

'Come on,' said the Glens, 'we'll show you the garden.'

The garden of Tamerlane Hall had hardly any flower beds in it, but as it was winter that did not matter much. I chiefly remember cedar trees and mown grass. The lawns went wandering away into the distance, and one could hardly tell where the garden ended and where the park and woods began.

The Glens took me on a tour of the objects of interest, starting with a sundial which was so complicated that we could not imagine how it worked. Then we visited the large stone lions which lurked in the shrubbery. Peggy said that they used to be on either side of the entry gate, but horses shied at them, so they had been taken down and hidden away where people seldom went and horses never. They looked so sad that we put a handful of leaves in their stone mouths.

Then we went to the grotto, where we felt rather nervous as the roof was unsafe and we were only supposed to go into it occasionally. It was a darkish underground room decorated with shells arranged in patterns. Thousands of shells must have been used and I should have liked to stay and have a really good look at it, only we were afraid to stop in it long because of the roof. Peter even said he thought he saw it wobbling.

'You wonder why anyone should bother to make it,' said Peggy as we came away. She was not romantic.

'Oh, but it's lovely,' I said. 'And perhaps there's a mystery to it.'

'Mr O'Sullivan says that it's a mystery how it's stayed up as long as it has,' said Peter.

On we went to the rubbish heap, which was one of the biggest and best rubbish heaps that I have ever had the good fortune to play on. In the middle was the life-sized statue of a Greek god who looked very cold standing there with arm outstretched above the dead leaves and decaying cabbage stalks.

'Why is he here?' I asked.

'Oh, don't you know?' said Peter. 'You've got to have one in a rubbish heap. Just *got* to.' He turned suddenly to Peggy. 'Isn't that the corner where you have your Secret Place?'

Peggy and Lionel had a very irritating habit of making Secret Places and then whispering about them. The rest of the children tried hard to discover where they were, but they never could, because whenever they guessed right the Secret Place was at once moved to somewhere else.

Peggy had had so many Secret Places that she could not quite remember if that particular corner of the rubbish heap was one or not.

'No, of course it isn't,' she said crossly.

Peter picked up a broken biscuit tin and looked inside. There were two old cartridges in it.

'It is! It is!' he cried.

Peggy became very bothered. She did not care about it herself but she knew that Lionel would be furious if she gave anything away.

'You're only a little squit,' she said. 'Squitty! Squitty! Squitty!'

'I'm not! I'm not!' shouted Peter, his angel face contorted with rage, and he rushed at her.

Peggy was much bigger than he was and she pushed him off easily. She was not quarrelsome by nature, and as Peter had entirely forgotten about the Secret Place she said peaceably,

'Let's go and look at the drawbridge.'

In one place the garden was divided from the park by a sunk fence which could be crossed by a plank which swung out from the wall on a hinge. We agreed to play at sieges, which was the game that was always played on it, but Peggy said:

'*Don't* let's be Cavaliers and Roundheads. Let's be the children in Nana's last place.'

Peter and I gladly agreed to this and we played happily at sieges for some time, even Marguerite being invited to join so as to make the sides even, though I don't think she at all understood what the game was about.

Presently Peter said:

'There's Grandpapa.'

We all stopped playing and stood and stared at a little procession coming slowly along one of the paths. In front walked a fox terrier; then came an old man in a bowler hat, leaning forward as he pulled the long handle of a bath chair behind him. The bath chair was pushed from the back by a hospital nurse in a bonnet and cape, and in it was a bundle of rugs and a coat and a cloth cap and I suppose a face, only I didn't really notice it.

The procession stopped when it came up to us and the old man who was pulling the chair seemed glad to straighten his back and stand upright. We talked a little to him and to the nurse and a lot to the dog who was called Pincher (which used to be a common name for dogs although it has now gone out of fashion).

When the procession had moved on again I asked:

'Which was Grandpapa?'

'I'm not quite sure if he was there,' said Peter.

'Of course he was, silly,' said Peggy. 'Do you think Pincher would have come out for a walk by himself?'

'Oh, he may have been under those rugs,' said Peter. 'It doesn't matter anyway.'

I expect Lord Tamerlane was really quite easy to see, but we weren't interested in him and so we hadn't bothered to look.

The stable clock struck three-quarters and we went back towards the house because at twelve o'clock we were always made to lie on our beds for an hour. It was known as 'resting', but I think the people who chiefly rested were the nurses. We were too old to sleep, and we weren't allowed to read, and the boredom for us children was really much more exhausting than ordinary play.

When we got near the house we found that two aunts had come out and had found Mrs Peabody's boomerang. They were taking it in turns to throw it, but they were not any cleverer than we had been, and the boomerang was going all over the place. They looked very funny, waving their arms and jerking their bodies, but they were nice, jolly aunts, and when we ran up and laughed at them, they laughed too. In fact everyone was having a good time when the smell of cigar told us that one of the men was bearing down on us.

'Don't look round,' muttered both the aunts together, but I did and saw coming towards me a bald head and bushy moustache. It was Aunt Muriel's Husband. For a ghastly moment I thought he had come to accuse Peggy and me, and I was just about to explain that it had all been Rosamund's idea when I saw that he was not looking at either of us. His eyes were fixed on the boomerang. I cheered up still more when I saw one of the aunts make a face at the other one, and I understood that they did not like him any more than we did.

'Well, it's a long time since I've had the pleasure of handling a boomerang,' said Aunt Muriel's Husband, stretching out his pudgy hand for it. 'Though of course when I was in Australia one got pretty used to the things.'

'It's Mrs Peabody's,' said one of the aunts, putting it behind her back. 'We're just going to return it to her.'

'I noticed you weren't being very successful with it,' said Aunt Muriel's Husband. 'I daresay you'd like me to show you how it's done.'

'Perhaps another time,' said the aunt, moving towards the house.

'Of course it's only a knack,' said Aunt Muriel's Husband, getting between her and the door. 'Some people pick it up very quickly and, on the other hand, of course, some people never seem able to get the hang of it. I happened to get the idea almost at once, that's all. In fact the natives were amazed. The first time I ever threw one was at a laughing jackass. As a matter of fact, that's a very amusing story. Did I ever tell you that story?'

'Yes,' said the aunt, rather rudely I thought. 'You have.'

'Well, since you all seem interested in boomerangs,' he went on, suddenly pulling it from her hand, 'I don't mind showing you just how it's done. Of course I haven't practised for years, but once you've got the knack you never absolutely lose it. Can the young idea see? I don't suppose really they'll pick it up – people don't often – but they may as well learn the right way of doing it. Now, it's a question of wrist, how you flick your wrist. They say there's a special shape of bone needed but I don't know about that. Well, what is it?'

Peter was standing right in front of him and stammering.

'D-do you think you ought to th-throw it? It's Mrs Peabody's. And she told us to take great care of it.'

Aunt Muriel's Husband laughed a loud hawhaw.

'Don't worry,' he said. 'I shouldn't suppose there are five other men now in England who have handled boomerangs as much as me. All you have to do is jerk it with the special flick of the wrist and it flies in a circle and comes safely back again into your own hand.'

A window in the house was opened and we saw Mrs Peabody looking out. He nodded to her and then flung the boomerang from him with great force. It whizzed through the air with the most desperate straightness, and crashing into the trunk of a cedar tree, smashed into smithereens.

'Crumbs,' said Peter.

5. Savage by Name and Savage by Nature

COMPARED to my calm schoolroom at home, the Tamerlane nursery was a very riotous place. The trouble was caused, needless to say, by the Savages. There were so many of them that even when most of them had decided to keep quiet, there would surely be one who felt like making a disturbance. Often, however, it was all of them together. I will tell you about my second teatime, and then you will see the sort of way in which they used to behave.

Harry was just finishing one of his stories which the other children half believed, although by that time they might have learnt that they were pure make-up.

'... Last year, when me and Mr O'Sullivan went shooting, he shot five and I shot fifty.'

'Fifty what?' asked Lionel.

'Birds,' said Harry, who did not know much natural history.

'Why didn't we see them?'

'We sent them to a hospital at once, so they wouldn't go bad.'

'Where is your gun?'

'Broken. I threw it away.'

'I don't believe you can shoot any more than a tomcat.'

'And I don't believe you can shoot any more than a William dog,' retorted Harry.

By this time they had settled down to tea and Nana Glen, pouring out at the big-children's table, told Harry to sit straight on his chair and not to gulp down his milk.

'Need I, Nana?' he asked, looking across at his own nurse at the centre table. She was busy cutting fingers of bread and butter for the baby and did not pay much attention.

'Harry always reminds me of the children of Israel eating the Passover in haste, with his loins girded and his staff in his hand,' she said indifferently.

Harry smirked triumphantly over the top of his cup and made a loud sucking noise. All the children giggled and the mouths of the nursery maids twitched. Nana Glen looked severe, specially when Betty spluttered her milk over the tablecloth.

'Hooray! Toast *and* strawberry jam,' said Rosamund, 'we can have Twixes.'

'Oh no, *not* Twixes,' and 'Yes, good, we'll have Twixes,' said Betty and Harry together.

'What are these Twixes?' I asked Lionel in my best society voice. I tried to hold my cup in two hands as I had sometimes seen my mother's visitors do, but Nana Glen said, 'Hold the handle, Evelyn, only babies hold their mugs that way. You're a big girl.'

'Twixes are bilge,' said Lionel.

'Sour dates,' retorted Harry. He really meant sour grapes but, as I have said, he was very bad at natural history.

'Twixes are little animals rather like squirrels,' explained Rosamund. 'Harry and I have them in our knives. If you spread strawberry jam on toast and then spread butter on the top of it, they make the mixture taste absolutely luscious.'

'Oh, I must try.'

'I'm afraid it's no use *your* trying,' said Harry, wagging his head and looking as though he were deeply grieved. 'You, poor soul, haven't got a Twix in *your* knife. Only me and Rosamund have got Twixes in our knives. I am sorry to say that if you try to do it, it will only taste quite ordinary. Not the real Twix taste.'

'Let me see your Twix,' I said. 'I don't believe you've got one.'

Harry stared into my eyes, and then said, still sadly and solemnly:

'As I feared. Quite the wrong sort of eyes. You'll never be able to see them. I was afraid you wouldn't be able to.'

I began to feel angry and tried to get Lionel on to my side, but he was busy with his own knife mixing butter and golden syrup into a cream which was called 'thunder and lightning' and made everything near it very sticky.

'They haven't got Twixes, have they, Lionel?'

'Of course they have. Excellent things Twixes. Always keep one handy. A Twix in time saves nine.'

'Betty hasn't got a Twix in her knife because she's too young,' said Rosamund.

Betty rose to the bait. 'It's all make-up,' she shouted. 'I don't believe it. You're untruth-tellers, both of you.'

'You wouldn't say that if you'd ever tasted Twix toast,' said Harry, who appeared to become sadder and sadder every moment. 'But you never have, and I don't suppose you ever will.'

Betty snatched Harry's knife away. 'Now I've got a Twix in my knife!'

Rosamund laughed a very put-on sort of laugh. 'I greatly fear the Twix ran out of it as soon as you picked it up.'

'It didn't! I can see it still there!' screamed Betty.

Harry peered closely at her knife and then shook his head. 'That's not a *real* Twix,' he said; 'that little misery couldn't make Twix toast.'

'I'll tell you what, Betty and Evelyn,' said Rosamund in a very kind and gentle voice which took in nobody, 'if you really want to know what Twix toast tastes like, let *me* spread some for you with *my* knife. I don't mind doing it a bit.'

But, of course, neither Betty nor I could stand that and there was a general clamour.

'Minnie says,' said Harry, 'that when Grand-mama can't make herself heard at a dinner party,

Grandpapa shouts down the table, 'Silence in the pig market. Let the old hen speak first.'

'Is that true, Minnie?'

'Of course,' said Minnie. 'She does, doesn't she, May?'

'Of course,' said May.

We had so little idea of what the grown-ups did when we weren't there that we believed her.

Lionel, who had gobbled up his thunder and lightning and was more or less covered with treacle, now stood up and said, 'Shall I show you a Chinese torture?'

Peter, who was next to him, said, 'Don't let him, Nana.'

'Lionel, sit down,' said Nana Glen.

'Peter, Peter, Pumpkin Eater. Had a wife and couldn't keep her. He put her in a pumpkin shell. And there he kept her very well,' chanted Lionel.

The other Savage children joined in, and I am sorry to say that Peggy and I couldn't help adding our voices to the uproar. The Howliboos began to whimper.

'I haven't. I didn't,' screamed poor Peter in a fury of rage, hitting out wildly at Lionel and sending a plate of scones flying.

'Lionel! Stop it this instant,' said Nana Glen, who loved Peter very much and didn't love Lionel at all.

'Pumpkin Eater! Pumpkin Eater!' shouted Lionel, standing on the sofa. The Howliboos were all howling together, Peter was screaming with rage and the rest of us were laughing and cheering.

Nana Glen sprang up, seized Lionel by the back of his collar and (I think) his hair and dragged him off the sofa and out of the room. She banged the door shut behind him and came back to her place grimly.

For a moment there was a surprised silence. The Howliboos turned their little heads about in relief and Baby Savage, who had been eating hard, flung both her buttery hands round her Nana's neck.

'If you love me tell me so, but don't grease my jacket,' said Nana Savage ungratefully, pushing her off and going on with her own tea.

'Really! Can no one control that boy?' said Nana Howliboo.

Neither of the other two nurses answered. Nana Glen was too cross and Nana Savage didn't care.

Crash! Besides the door into the passage, the nursery had two other doors leading into bedrooms.

Lionel had tiptoed through the sacred Howliboo night nursery and now bounced in upon us again screaming, 'Pumpkin Eater! Pumpkin Eater!'

The nursery maids rose from their places and chased him out, but as fast as they slammed one door behind him he rushed in at another. There were no keys, and he tore through the room again and again, the nursery maids trying to hold the doors but never knowing which he was going to attack next. In the middle of the uproar, and just as Lionel had thrown a cushion into the middle of the food, there came a heavy knock on the door which led into the passage.

No one had heard any footsteps so we all jumped, and Lionel popped under the table where he was well hidden by the long tablecloth.

Slowly, slowly the door opened and, to our astonishment, who should come in but Father Christmas.

We big ones naturally guessed at once that it must be someone dressed up; but it didn't look like anyone we knew and it did look exactly like Father Christmas. Betty was sitting opposite to me and I saw her round face go absolutely white as if she were about to faint, while Peter blushed purple.

'It's Mr O'Sullivan,' said Rosamund uncertainly. 'Or is it . . . ? Can it be . . . ?'

Father Christmas now raised his hand and began counting the children in a queer deep voice.

'One, two, three, four, five, six, seven, eight, nine, ten . . . ten?' Here he stopped. As Lionel was under the table of course we were one short. Father Christmas counted again, but it still came to ten.

Then he pronounced in a slow, solemn voice:

> *The child under the table,*
> *I give you fair warning,*
> *Will find nothing in his stocking*
> *On Christmas morning.'*

This was too much for Lionel who suddenly scrambled out and slunk on to his chair, trying to pretend he had been there all the time.

'Eleven!' said Father Christmas and slipped out of the room, shutting the door behind him.

'Quick!' cried Rosamund. 'Which way did he go?'

There was a rush to the door, but by the time we had got it open there was no one to be seen in the passage.

'I think it was Mr O'Sullivan,' said Rosamund again.

'I think it was Grandmama,' said Peggy.

'Grandmama doesn't have a beard.'

'Neither does Mr O'Sullivan.'

'If it wasn't really Father Christmas,' said Peter, 'how did he know that Lionel was under the table?'

How, indeed? We were all puzzled and turned to the grown-ups.

'Nana, who was it?' 'Minnie, May, who was it?' 'You've *got* to tell us who it was.'

But they only laughed, and I can't tell you anything more about it because the mystery was never solved.

The next disturbance came when we were getting ready to go downstairs. It was Betty being tiresome, and she chose to do it with her bedroom door open so as to attract as much attention as possible.

This was rather a way of hers and was considered very unsporting by the others. Betty and Rosamund always wore either pink or blue sashes on their white frocks, and Rosamund had dressed first and had put on the pink sash which had been laid ready for her. Suddenly Betty said that she couldn't wear pink, she wouldn't wear pink, nothing in the world would make her wear pink. Nana Savage would probably have given in, only Rosamund would not, of course, change to blue, and if they had gone downstairs with different sashes awkward questions would have been asked. Besides, Betty was shouting so loudly that everyone was hearing about it. 'Oh, very well,' said Nana Savage, 'go down and ask your mother if you need wear pink.'

Bold as brass, Betty stumped off downstairs, followed by the rest of us longing to see what would happen. The library looked even grander than before, the grown-ups round the fire seemed even older and more remote.

However, Betty walked down the middle of the room in a very don't-care way and, when she got to the circle of elders, said in the coarse voice which she used when she wanted to assert herself:

'Need I wear a pink sash? I 'ates pink.'

Her mother, who was among the group of ladies, said:

'Oh, Betty! Don't talk like a fishwife.'

Betty put on an aggrieved whine.

'But I don't know what a fish knife talks *like*.'

There was a sort of rustle among the ladies, but Betty's mother said seriously:

'Why don't you like pink?'

'Because,' replied Betty, frowning at her angrily, 'it upsets my applecart.'

At this there was a loud roar – a roar of laughter really, only Betty took it to be a roar of rage. She thought she must have gone too far this time and have said something really terrible. Suddenly losing her nerve, she turned and bolted out of the library.

When she returned later on it was with a very red face and a pink sash.

That evening our games were organized by the youngest uncle who was called Uncle Jack. They were nice games, as they didn't need any practice, and even I could play them as well as anyone.

We finished up with one called bullet pudding. There was a heap of flour on a plate and a marble on the top of it, and we all took turns to cut a slice off the flour with a knife. The heap of flour got smaller and smaller until it collapsed altogether and the marble rolled into the flour. Then the person who had knocked it down had to pick up the marble in his teeth, and if you can, without dribbling, bury your face in a heap of flour and pick up a marble between your teeth, you are cleverer than we were. Our faces and hair were soon plastered with dough and the din was terrific. Betty was giving her famous screams – when she was excited she always screamed like a train going through a tunnel. The grown-ups, who were standing round us, laughed, too, Lady Tamerlane as much as anyone. She was a person who hardly ever said 'Don't'. Having herself been one of a family of fifteen she was resigned to the behaviour of children.

When we got back upstairs the nurses took a very different line. Even Nana Savage was startled from her usual calm when she saw us coming in with our faces whitened like clowns.

'Look at yourselves!' she said. 'They wouldn't accept you in the workhouse.'

'I don't want to be accepted in the workhouse,' said Rosamund pertly.

'Hadn't somebody better start running the bathwater?' said Harry primly. He was fascinated by the weighing-machine in the bathroom.

The nursery wing was lucky in having a bathroom of its own, but using it was a serious undertaking, as the water came out of the tap in a thin red trickle, and it took a long time to get enough water for even a shallow bath. The other peculiarity of the bathroom was that round the wall ran an extremely hot pipe which one forgot about until one bumped into it.

'If I'd known they were going to play that dirty game,' said Nana Glen, 'I wouldn't have put Peter in his black velvet.'

Nana Howliboo, whose babies were safely in bed, smiled like a Cheshire cat.

'Once velvet is soiled you can't ever remove the marks,' she said. 'I'd never put a boy in velvet myself.'

'You may think everything is all wrong,' explained Harry earnestly, 'but everything is really all right. Uncle Jack made us do it.'

'Then Uncle Jack should know better at his age,' said Nana Glen.

'What is Uncle Jack's age?' said Rosamund. 'Is he older than you or younger than you?' She had a craving to find out the nurses' real ages, rather as though it would give her some magic hold over them. But Nana Glen was not to be drawn and merely snorted.

'And Grandmama egged him on,' said Peggy.

'She stood beside him, she really did, and said "Capital!" and "Bravo!" '

'Your grandmama's past praying for,' said Nana Glen, but wasting no further words she sent her nursery maid to seize and hold the bathroom. Lionel had got there first, however, and was wiping the dough off his face with Peter's bath towel.

'Nana's coming,' remarked the nursery maid as she turned on the tap.

'Put Peter's towel down *at once*,' said Nana Glen bustling in.

'Isn't it mine?' said Lionel. 'Oh, a thousand apologies. Bad mistake to take somebody else's bath towel, specially a Pumpkin Eater's. Mustn't occur again. Where shall I put it? Sweets to the sweet and bath towels to the bath.' So saying he flung the towel into the water and skipped out of the door. 'Ow!' he cried as he burnt his leg on the hot pipe.

6. Christmas Eve

'QUICK! Quick!' cried Rosamund who was looking out of the nursery window. 'What do you think is going in at the front door!'

It was after breakfast and Nana Howliboo had opened the windows to air the room and had ordered us to go away; but Rosamund had collected us again and told us to come back. She loved a feud, and as her own Nana was too lazy to fight for herself she felt it was her duty to annoy Nana Howliboo whenever an opportunity offered.

Everybody ran to the open window and hung out as well as the bars and rabbit-netting would allow.

'Betty's not to see it,' said Rosamund, suddenly turning elder-sisterly, and she flung herself on

Betty and put her hands over her eyes. Betty, not unnaturally, fought like a wild animal, snarling, writhing and kicking. 'Only donkeys kick,' said Rosamund.

For a change Betty bit Rosamund, who was so surprised that she let go her hold and Betty dashed to the window.

'I've seen it! It's the tree!'

The tree was such a big one that the gardeners were having great difficulty in getting it through the front door. Mr O'Sullivan was out on the gravel giving directions, and there was a crowd of men – the odd man in a green baize apron and the house carpenter in a white one, and others whose names we did not know. We waved and shouted to them, leaning out of the window which Nana Howliboo had so kindly opened.

'Don't fall out,' shouted Mr O'Sullivan jokingly.

This gave Rosamund an idea.

'Let's play an April Fool on Nana Howliboo,' she said. 'Let's pretend that Betty has fallen out of the window. She can hide behind the curtains and cry aloud for help, and we can arrange her shoes with the soles upwards as though she were just hanging on by her toes.'

'But no one could really fall out,' said someone, 'because of the bars and the rabbit-netting.'

'In her frenzy Nana Howliboo will forget about the bars,' said Rosamund.

She was right. The April Fool was a perfect success. We put Betty's shoes on the windowsill with a cushion which happened to be much the same colour as Betty's dress, and then rolled Betty up in the curtain so that she was completely hidden.

Very softly we went out into the passage but left the door open, and then Betty let out the most frightful yells for help. They would have taken in anyone. The night-nursery door burst open and Nana Howliboo came charging out and dashed to the window exclaiming:

'Oh, my godfathers!'

Nana Glen whizzed in from the other side.

Then, of course, the rest of us rushed in too, and danced about shouting, 'April Fool!'

The nurses, having had a bad fright, were not at all pleased, but there was nothing that they could do about it, and fortunately at that moment the odd man came in and dumped on the floor a dust-sheet full of holly, yew and box. The nurses stopped glaring at us and turned and glared at each other. Then both clawed at the pile and took up an armful of greenery which they carried away to their bedrooms.

They were back in a moment, confronting each other across the dust-sheet. Who was going to decorate the day nursery?

Rosamund, seeing that Nana Savage was taking no part, snatched up an armful, too, and the Savages ran off to decorate their bedroom. I, however, had been nicely brought up.

'Please can I have some for my room?' I asked politely.

'I'm afraid not, dear,' said Nana Howliboo. 'There isn't too much left for the day nursery as it is – not so as to do it properly.' She squinted at Nana Glen, who said:

'Take as much as you like, dear.' She gave me all I could carry, so much, in fact, that I had some over to give to Marguerite.

When I got back to the nursery I found that Nana Howliboo had lost the day, as her babies had started howling and she had had to go off to see to them.

The Glen nursery maid was standing on a chair while Nana Glen was handing her bits of holly with exact directions how to place each one, mixed with complaints that the gardener thought any old rubbish good enough for the nursery. It took some time, as they had to put a strip of greenery along the top of every single picture. There were fourteen pictures in the nursery, as I remember very well. One was of the Russian Army looking at Constantinople, one was of Chinese ladies having tea on the floor and the other twelve were of volcanoes. Some of the volcanoes only had a little wisp of smoke at the top, others had smoke and fire, while in the best one the sky was a sheet of flame and people in boats were fleeing for their lives.

After the pictures were finished, paper festoons were produced and stretched across the room so thickly that you could hardly see the ceiling. Just as the last of these was being fastened Nana Howliboo came back and looked around her with contempt.

'Isn't it glorious!' said Rosamund, reappearing again through one of the other doors. Nana Howliboo knew quite well that she was only saying this to be annoying, so she replied:

'Run along, dear, and get ready to go out. And tell Minnie to brush your hair. It looks a perfect sight.'

That morning it was the Glens' turn to go out riding, and I went for a walk with the four Savages and some nursery maids.

'Let's tell story,' they said as soon as we started. So we walked along in a row and the Savages 'told story', which meant that they chattered away about the adventures of themselves and a lot of imaginary people with Greek and Roman names who endlessly fought battles and killed each other. You might have imagined it difficult for four people to tell the same story at the same time, but the Savages managed it; in fact, they quarrelled less over their story than over anything else. I, on the other hand, found it impossible to join in as, to begin with, I couldn't make any sense of it at all, and to go on with, whenever I got tired of keeping silence and ventured a suggestion, the others shut me up.

'Oh, no, Evelyn. He couldn't have done that.'

'But why couldn't he? Your people seem able to do anything.'

'You don't understand.'

I didn't understand, and I thought their story frightfully boring, and I told them so; but they went on with it just the same. I tried walking with the nursery maids, but the four children gabbling away drew me as a magnet draws a needle and I kept going back to them. Their story, as far as I could make it out, was as silly as possible. It was all about their imaginary countries which must have been very unpleasant places to live in. Wars were nonstop and you never could get rid of your wicked men, as when anyone died they went to a place in the clouds called Fairyland, and every month lifts came down from Fairyland to Earth. Sometimes you killed a person just before a lift was due to start, and there he was back again in two twos. Of course, if you were killed yourself, you also could come alive again; but on the whole Fairyland seemed a bad arrangement.

'Oh, do stop and talk about something interesting,' I said. 'Let me tell you about the Pageant I saw last summer.'

'You don't understand,' they said, and went on telling story.

In the afternoon everyone went down to the farm in a swarm. Fathers and mothers, uncles and aunts came too. The Savages buzzed round their father who was a large, silent man who liked children. The children asked him questions the whole time.

'Dada,' said Harry, 'is Grandpapa ninety?'

'No.'

'But, Dada, he said he could remember the Battle of Navarino, which was in 1827, you know, and if he could really *remember* it, he must be ninety.'

'You shouldn't muddle his old brain.'

'Dada, was Hannibal a better general than Julius Caesar?'

'Comparisons are odious.'

'Dada,' said Lionel, 'if a dinosaur fought a pterodactyl who would win?'

'Dada,' said Harry, 'which would win if a Gurkha and a Zouave fought two Zulus?'

'Dada,' said Betty, 'who would win, Mr O'Sullivan or an elephant with a Gatling gun?'

'Dada,' said Rosamund, whose front teeth were already missing, 'do look in my mouth. I believe I've got another tooth loose.'

'How sharper than a serpent's thanks it is to have a toothless child,' said her father. His remarks were apt to be mystifying, and we all meditated for a moment on what a serpent's thanks would be like. However, silence did not last, and soon they were all quarrelling as to whether Betty could go into the Army when she grew up.

'Can.'

'Can't.'

'Can.'

'You're only a silly little girl.'

'Silly little girl yourself.'

'Dada, she can't, can she?'

'Dada, I can, can't I?'

'Don't cross your bridges till you come to them,' said their father. I tried to exchange amused glances with him, but he strode along with his head bent and his eyes on the ground. To attract his attention I said:

'Look at that man over there. How lazy he is to walk so slowly.'

'The ploughman homeward plods his weary way,' said the Savages' father. 'How many different ways can you say that?'

We all began shouting at once, 'The homeward weary ploughman plods his way,' and 'His weary way the ploughman homeward plods,' and so on. No one could keep count of the different ways of saying it, and it lasted as a topic the rest of the way to the farm.

In the barn there was a crowd of men and women and a great heap of raw meat. The people came up one by one to Lady Tamerlane (Lord

Tamerlane's bath chair was there but he took no part) and she said a few words to each of them. At the same time a chunk of meat was handed to them by a man who had a hook instead of a hand, like Captain Hook in *Peter Pan*. We none of us could take our eyes off that hook as it flashed among the meat, cleverly hooking out exactly the right joint for everybody.

When we started back, the Savages' father went with their mother to call on one of the cottages, so Betty said: 'I think I will walk with Pincher and his crew,' and marched off beside Lord Tamerlane's bath chair.

'I shall walk with Marguerite,' said Harry. 'I talk to her in Old English.'

'Do you mean Anglo-Saxon?' asked his grandmother.

'Yes,' said Harry. 'It sounds awful nonsense to me but she likes it.' He started spouting gibberish and Marguerite really seemed quite pleased by his attentions.

I looked for a grown-up to attach myself to, but they all seemed to be busy talking to each other, so I had to put up with Rosamund.

'Shall I say you some poetry?' she said, and started gabbling away before I could stop her.

'*Queen Sigrid the haughty sat proud and aloft.*'

'If she was a queen why did she sit in a loft?' I asked.

'Don't interrupt,' said Rosamund, and went gabbling on. Every now and then she seemed to come to the end of a poem, for she would put her head on one side and in a slow, soppy voice say:

> '*The eternal dawn, beyond a doubt,*
> *Shall break on hill and plain,*
> *And put all stars and candles out,*
> *Ere we be young again.*'

Then she would start gabbling on as fast as before.

By the time we reached home she had said the soppy bit so often that we both felt like old, old women and could hardly drag our boots up the stairs. However, by tea time we had become sufficiently young again to play a joke on Lionel. He was late and Nana Glen had poured out his tea and Rosamund and I put jam in it and also mustard, salt and pepper (the cruet was on the table because there was hot buttered toast). The grown-ups pretended not to notice, but I could see that Nana Glen and the nursery maids were watching when he picked up his cup. The stuff had sunk to the bottom so Lionel did not realize that there was anything wrong till he was halfway down and then he got it all together in one gulp.

'Pumpkin Eater yourself,' cried Peter in delight as Lionel coughed and spluttered.

That evening, when we were dressed and ready, we did not go down the dragon stairs as usual, but down the little blue stairs which landed one near Lady Tamerlane's sitting room. This mysterious apartment was sometimes called the Chinese Room. The wallpaper was patterned with Chinese flowers, and on the ceiling were painted clouds with a dragon (more dragons!) flying among them. The furniture was got up to look like bamboo, and the carpet was so thick that the footsteps of even the noisiest child could not be heard. A special warm, exciting smell always hung in the air, and more exciting still, there was at one side a sort of alcove draped with silk hangings. It made a little dark passage with cushioned seats at the side, and at the end were glass doors.

As soon as we got into Lady Tamerlane's sitting room there was a scurry for the alcove and the glass doors. Ourselves in deep shadow, we looked through into the ballroom, which was blazing with light from dozens of candles. In the middle stood an immense Christmas tree, glittering, sparkling, dazzling.

'O-o-ooh!' we all said.

My memory of the rest of the evening is rather confused. I can see us joining hands and dancing round the tree, and I can see Mr O'Sullivan walking about with a sponge on the end of a long stick with which he put out any dangerous candles, and I can see a work basket lined with red satin which I suppose was my present, and I can see the fairy doll at the top which I wanted but didn't get – no one got it – and I can see the servants crowding in at a side door and coming up one by one to receive a roll of dark cloth from Lady Tamerlane – each bobbed low as she took her roll and then the next one came forward.

And then somehow we were upstairs again in the twilight of our bedrooms eating our suppers and chattering. We all had a glass of milk, and a ginger biscuit and a marie biscuit, which could either be eaten one at a time or together like a sandwich. Both ways made a lot of crumbs.

Peggy ran into my room to swap her marie for my ginger and I ran into hers to borrow a big safety-pin (you can probably guess what for). Marguerite had remembered to pack one of my father's stockings but not a safety-pin. However, Nana Glen had quantities of them, and my brass bedrail was just the shape I needed.

Then I heard the Savages giggling so much that I had to run into their room to see what was happening. Harry had fallen out of bed and Nana Savage had said, 'Get back to bed, you silly little fellow,' but he continued to lie on the floor, laughing and unable to move. The nurses were all rather keen to hurry us along, as later in the evening there was to be dancing. (In the housekeeper's room the music was provided by Mr O'Sullivan who played the violin, and in the servants' hall there was a sort of barrel organ.)

But, before that, mothers had to come round to hear prayers and say goodnight. As I hadn't a mother Lady Tamerlane heard my prayers, which she did in the brisk businesslike way that she did everything. She carried a special candlestick with a glass funnel to protect the flame as she moved swiftly down the corridor, and she went round the children and kissed them in turn.

Then our own candles were blown out and we were left lying in the dark to wait for Father Christmas. We were all excited but in different ways, from Tommy who was so horrified and revolted by the idea of a dreadful old man coming down the chimney in the middle of the night that they had had to hang his stocking outside his door, to Lionel who had put a wet sponge beside his bed with the worst intentions. I was in that state when you don't know what to expect or whom to believe, and I several times crept to the end of my bed to feel my limp stocking. Was it possible that in a few hours' time that dingy woollen object would be oozing toys?

Just as I was dropping off to sleep I was roused by the sound of the Savages' door being violently thrown open and bare feet pattering along the passage.

'Nana!' wailed Harry, 'Minnie! May! *My stocking's empty! There's nothing in it!*'

Loud unfeeling laughter burst from the nursery and presently Harry was led back to bed by Minnie, who explained gently that though he had been asleep, it wasn't morning.

I was glad Harry had made such a disturbance as I had been getting very drowsy myself and I did really mean to lie awake till Father Christmas came so as to settle once and for all *who* he was. But the room was pitch dark except for a strip of light under the door, and it was very difficult to keep my eyes open. I could not see the pictures of stags but I wondered what they would think of reindeer. 'Is Father Christmas a Cavalier or a Roundhead? And suppose he has hooks instead of hands, and hooks instead of feet, and wears a pink sash . . .'

7. Christmas Day

PRESENTLY I noticed that the crack of light wasn't there any more, and as I lay in the dark I became aware of a strong smell of oranges. Vaguely I wondered where the smell was coming from and then, with a start, I asked myself, could it be coming from my stocking?

Regardless of the cold, I pushed back the bedclothes and crawled to the end of my bed and my hand met something that was woolly, hard and sharp. Nothing else in the world feels quite like a well-stuffed stocking.

My hand followed the bumps and jags up to the top and there the woolliness ended and I could feel something which in the darkness I mistook for the top of an umbrella – it afterwards turned out to be a book. With a sigh of relief I nipped back under the bedclothes thinking, 'The Magic has worked yet once again. He has come.'

We had been told not to get up till half past six and Rosamund had promised to call me so that we could all unpack together. I wondered what the time was, and at that moment the stable clock obligingly struck. I counted fourteen, which seemed strange and exciting, but on thinking it over I decided that I must have added in the chimes and that it was really six. To have to wait for half an hour was almost unbearable, but there seemed nothing else to be done, specially as I had no matches. I tried to lie still but the stocking seemed to pull me towards it, and every few minutes I was down at the end of my bed feeling to make sure that there was no mistake.

At last the stable clock struck half past and my door was flung open by Rosamund. She was carrying a candle and her hair was in three pigtails tied up with rags.

'Happy Christmas!' she shouted in a voice loud enough to wake the whole of Tamerlane. 'Happy Christmas! Happy Christmas!'

In an instant I was up and had unpinned my stocking which suddenly became so heavy that I dropped it on the floor. I then saw that there were things on the chair as well. I tried not to look to see what they were as I grabbed the lot and then had to lay them down again as I put on my dressing gown.

When I got to Rosamund's room I found the other children were already there.

'Two candles aren't enough,' said Lionel, 'and Minnie says that three is very unlucky. Fetch all your candles, Evelyn, and we'll have a grand illumination.'

'All right, only nobody must look at anything till I come back.'

So I fetched my candles, and when Rosamund had lit them by tipping a lighted one against them (the grease ran down on to the carpet but we didn't mind) the room looked very gay. We huddled together on to the beds and Rosamund commanded:

'Everybody to pull out together and only one thing at a time. Are you all ready? Now! One, two, three, go!'

I am afraid I have forgotten most of the things that came out of those stockings, except that Rosamund and I each got a clock. Hers was red and mine was blue, and they were called Bee clocks. They stood on little legs which we soon found could be unscrewed, and then the case came to pieces and the glass fell out and all the works could be seen. I also had a set of teeny little flower pots about two inches high. There was a teeny watering can with them and packets of mustard and cress seed. Later on when I was back in London I followed the directions with the help of my governess and the mustard and cress did actually grow and we ate it for tea.

But the thing that pleased me most was a glass swan exactly like Mrs Peabody's, except that while hers had red eyes, mine had green. I could hardly believe that it had come to me already, without having to wait till I was grown up. I kissed it and put it beside my bed, next to my Bible, though not on top of it, as that would have been irreverent.

After breakfast I was told to go with the Savages to their mother's room where I should find the presents which my parents had sent for me. As we raced along the passage a frantic quarrel broke out between Rosamund and Harry as to which of them was to be given an annual called *Little Folks*.

The Savages' mother had set out five chairs with heaps of presents on each and we pounced down on them, Betty of course with a terrific squeal. I found that my presents were just what I wanted but what I thought I should never be given – beyond that I can't describe them.

Presents poured in at intervals throughout the day, but the only one I can remember is a life-sized dachshund on wheels. Great-Uncle Algy gave it to Tommy, who at once broke into such howls of terror that it was quickly handed on to me who happened to be standing near. I had got past the age when people usually give you stuffed animals, so I was very pleased to get this one. He was christened Great Agrippa and went to bed with me for years.

At one moment we all surged down into the dining room where the uncles and aunts were having their breakfast. One got to the dining room by going through a mysterious little room full of doors which was known as the lobby and had a black-and-white marble floor and buffaloes' horns on the wall. One opened the biggest door and found oneself behind a screen, and when one had walked round the end of the screen one found oneself in an immense room with pillars in it. The grown-ups were eating at a big table in the middle, but there were wide open spaces all round them and other tables near the walls. With a whoop the Savages dashed towards a large polished table which stood in the corner and began playing ships on it and under it. I took in the situation at a glance and decided to follow an idea of my own and to go to the grown-up table where the people breakfasting would be at my mercy. I spotted an uncle whom I had not seen before and who I thought would find me irresistible, and I felt contempt for the Savages who were so childish that they chose to play ships under the sideboard at a time when they might have been fascinating the house party.

Unfortunately for my plans, on my way towards my victim I had to pass near a table on which was a boar's head. The boar had rolling eyes and great tusks and I suppose was really only an ordinary pig, but it looked like something out of history. Round it was mashed jelly of a beautiful golden colour, and as no one was looking at me I stuck two fingers in and took a great mouthful.

Then I was in a fix indeed. The jelly was perfectly horrible and I couldn't possibly bring myself to swallow it, but I didn't dare to spit it out. Instead of going to fascinate the grown-ups I had to slink into the corner after the other children.

'Come up on deck, Evelyn,' said Rosamund, stretching out a hand.

But I ducked down into the cabin, where I found Harry and Peter.

'Which will you be,' said Harry, 'stoker or stewardess?' The Savages sometimes went to Ireland and so they knew about ships.

I nodded, still unable to open my mouth.

'What does that senseless sort of nod mean?' asked Harry. 'Does it mean you want to be a stoker and shovel coal till the perspiration pours off you in rivers, or does it mean that you want to be a stewardess and hand round basins?'

It really meant that I wished somebody would hand *me* a basin, but at that moment the captain's head appeared upside down as he leant over from the deck, and while Harry and Peter were exchanging remarks with it, I managed to get rid of the jelly under the corner of the carpet which was fortunately not nailed down.

'I think I'll just be a passenger,' I said, 'a grand lady with lots of luggage and a Pomeranian.'

'What class are you going?' asked Harry:

'First-class cabin full of shoes,
Second-class cabin hullabaloos,
Third-class cabin full of oats
    [for the animals],
Fourth-class cabin full of boats
    [that's really the top deck and it's frightfully
cold and always rains].'

I said I should certainly go first class. Peter now began shovelling coal, and considering that the coal, the shovel and the furnace were all imaginary, he somehow managed to produce very loud and lifelike noises. I looked out of a porthole to see how the grown-ups were bearing it, but they were so wrapped up in themselves and their own breakfasts that they did not seem to notice us at all.

'Land ahoy!' shouted Lionel's voice from the deck. 'Stop the ship! We're running on to a rock! Stop her, can't you, you donkeys.'

'Very sorry, Captain,' shouted Rosamund. 'Afraid I can't! The wheel's stuck.'

'Stand by for a wreck!' shouted Lionel. 'Man the boats! Women and children first!' Here he threw Betty into the sea. She let out one of her most horrible yells and came rolling into the cabin.

'Rock's getting closer, getting closer,' shouted Lionel. 'Now I can see the houses, now I can see the people, now I can see the gulls, now I can see the winkles. And now for the beastly bump.'

As he spoke the three children on the deck crashed over together and there were shouts of 'Take to the boats!' 'Swim for your lives!' and also, less appropriately, 'Fire! Murder! Burglary!'

The whole lot of us (myself among them) were now swimming about on the carpet, but Lady Tamerlane had finished her breakfast.

'Run on, children, and get ready for church,' she said as she rose from the table, and as no one ever thought of disobeying her, up we got and off we ran.

Getting ready for church took us a long time, particularly as the nurses could not agree as to whether we were to wear our Sunday clothes or not. I think in the end we wore our Sunday coats but not our Sunday hats, but somehow we were made to feel just as stiff and uncomfortable as if we were dressed entirely in Sunday outfits.

Ding, dong, dell, went the church bells.

'Hurry up, Harry,' said Nana Savage languidly. 'There are the bells saying "Come-to-church! Come-to-church!"'

We stopped to listen, but at that moment the peal changed to Dinga-dinga-dong.

'But now they are saying "Go-a-way-from-church! Go – a – way – from – church!"' objected Harry.

We were shocked by Harry, and still more so by Betty who announced that she was going to take her bear to church. Indeed, this made us really anxious, as it was almost impossible to get Betty to change her mind once she had made it up, but to the relief of everybody she came to her senses in time. She said that after all she had decided that Bear was rather young for church, so instead she would leave him sitting on the dirty-clothes basket so that he could have a nice cosy talk to it with no one listening.

'And what does the clothes-basket talk about?' asked Mrs Peabody, who had drifted in.

Betty gave Mrs Peabody a suspicious look to see if her leg was being pulled.

'It talks about nothing but clothes,' she said.

Eventually we got off and went in a straggling crowd down the avenue. The church stood by itself in the park, a little old church with cedar trees in the churchyard. The grass was neatly mown and the path was weeded and the graves were decorated with holly wreaths. Beside it was a big mound covered with trees which the children called the giant's castle. We never got the chance to explore it, so for all I know a giant really did live on top.

In church we filled several pews, the children being put in one against the back wall, which was a good thing as a great deal of whispering and giggling went on. I think children don't giggle as much now as they used to, perhaps because they are not so strictly brought up. When we were all in the pew a ledge on a hinge was fixed across the opening so as to make more room and the child who knelt in front of that was always pushing his prayer book over it or else just catching it in time. In either case the rest of us giggled.

Peter and Betty shared a prayer book. They followed the service closely, and whenever they came to a word they could read they joined in as loudly as they could. Peter showed Betty what 'Amen' looked like and they waited panting for every one and then bawled it, generally coming in a second too soon or a second too late. Rosamund's prayer book was full of pretty little markers which kept slipping out and fluttering to the ground, followed by dives and head-bumping.

Harry behaved fairly well although he occasionally asked questions in his usual voice without making any attempt to lower it, while Lionel behaved beautifully except during the hymns. These he would sing to ridiculous words which he had picked up at school and which we all thought terribly witty.

I was in two minds whether to sit primly like the grown-ups or to wriggle and giggle like the children, and I tried first one way and then the other. Unfortunately Lady Tamerlane chose to look round just as I was laughing at Peggy waggling her finger through a hole in her glove, and she made me come out of the back pew and sit beside her for the rest of the service. I was covered with shame at this public disgrace and thought that everyone in the church, from the clergyman to the old man who blew the organ, was looking at me with scorn.

However, I recovered my spirits on the way home, as one of the great-aunts walked beside me and talked to me as though nothing had happened. She told me stories of what she and her cousins had done when they were young and I came to the conclusion that Victorian children, far from being little angels, were really much naughtier than we were. It was astonishing to learn that Great-Uncle

Algy had mesmerized his governess and had then not been able to un-mesmerize her again, or that Lady Tamerlane herself had, when a little girl, gone into a visitor's bedroom and put soapy water in all her cupboards and drawers as a suggestion that she was staying too long. 'And once,' said the great-aunt in her little squeaky voice, 'we all decided to run away.'

I couldn't help laughing. We had dropped behind the others, as the great-aunt could hardly walk, and the idea of her running at all was absurd.

'Where were you going to run to?'

'We meant either to go to London to be crossing-sweepers, or to Malvern because the water was so good.'

'And what happened?'

'Gustavus always was a tell-tale-tit,' said the great-aunt, her dim eyes flashing as she looked at the bent back of an aged gentleman tottering along in front of us. I could see that she never had quite forgiven him for sneaking.

By the time I reached the house I had entirely got back my good opinion of myself and was able to eat as much turkey and Christmas pudding as anybody.

8. Boxing Day

I HAVE often noticed that one feels rather flat on Boxing Day. The weather is generally grey and dull, and children are apt to be tired and bored.

'I can't think why it is,' said Rosamund, 'I don't really like these sweets at all now, and yet I just can't stop eating them.'

'My mouth feels all sugary inside,' I said, 'I wonder if one of those lumps of nougat would take the taste away.'

I took one but it was horrid, and when I tried to throw it into the fire it hit the fender. It became very runny and stuck in the wire meshes, and the more we tried to poke it through with a pencil the more sticky everything became.

'You'd better not have any more sweets, Harry,' said Rosamund, 'not after what happened at dinner.'

Harry appeared to be pondering great thoughts. At last he spoke.

'Sick can be very surprising sometimes.'

'Well, we certainly were more surprised than pleased,' said Rosamund. 'Why did you say that you were too hungry to eat?'

'Because I thought I was,' said Harry humbly.

We were interrupted by Lady Tamerlane coming in to suggest that the nursery maids should take us down to the back lodge to watch the Marathon race.

'And which of you can tell me what a Marathon race is?' she asked.

Lionel would certainly have known, but he wasn't there and so we all looked at Rosamund, hoping that she would rise to the occasion.

'It is a race,' said Rosamund bravely, 'run by Marathons, who are, who were, a sort of ancient Greek.'

'Or is it something to eat,' suggested Peter, 'like an egg-and-spoon race?'

'Have none of you really ever heard of Marathon?' asked Lady Tamerlane, delighted to have an excuse for telling us about it.

'I have,' I spoke up, seeing my chance to score off the others and impress a grown-up at last. 'I know Marathon very well. We always start from Marathon Station when we go to stay with Aunt Mildred.'

'Marylebone Station, I expect,' said Lady Tamerlane, not, alas, impressed. 'Well, I see I shall have to tell you the story of Marathon.'

This roused Betty. She came out from under the sofa and stood in front of her grandmother.

'Are there any fairies in it?' she asked suspiciously. 'Because if there are, it's not true.'

'There are no fairies in the story of Marathon,' said Lady Tamerlane.

'That's a blooming good thing,' said Betty.

Lady Tamerlane looked as if she would like to criticize this remark but changed her mind and began.

'Marathon was one of the decisive battles of the world.'

'Which are the other ones?' Harry asked.

'I will tell you that later,' said his grandmother, who was never at a loss for an answer and who had plenty of encyclopaedias downstairs, 'or better still, you children might all make lists of decisive battles.'

'Go on, Grandmama,' said Peggy quickly.

'Well, Greece was in dire peril. It was being invaded by the mighty armies of the Persians who were coming by way of the Plain of Marathon, between the mountains and the sea. The mountains look on Marathon and Marathon looks on the sea.'

'Exactly how far is Marathon from Navarino?' asked Harry.

'The Battle of Marathon and the Battle of Navarino are separated by over two thousand years,' said Lady Tamerlane who, as I said before, was never at a loss for an answer, and had had plenty of practice with children. 'Although the Persians far outnumbered the Greeks, the Greeks it was who conquered. They rushed down upon the Persians and won a great victory. Then the question arose, who should carry the good tidings to Athens? And the choice fell on Pheidippides, a swift runner who had already run to Sparta and back and had also fought bravely in the battle.'

'What a funny person to choose,' said Peggy, who did not much care for history but thought that somebody ought to say something.

Lady Tamerlane gave a quick glance at Betty who was standing there glowering. Although it is strictly true that there are no fairies in the story of

Marathon, what about that bit when Pheidippides has a talk with the Great God Pan? Lady Tamerlane was not at all sure that Betty would approve of the Great God Pan and so decided that there was not really time to mention him. So she went straight on –

'Pheidippides ran swiftly to Athens and told them that the country was saved. And then down he dropped, dead.'

Betty turned away. No fairies had been mentioned and she was disappointed.

'What was the point of running so fast?' said Harry. 'If they had lost the battle there would have been some sense in it. But as they had won it, what was the hurry?'

'So nowadays,' said Lady Tamerlane, frankly taking no notice, 'very long races are called Marathon races.'

'And I suppose everyone has to drop down dead at the end of them,' said Harry. 'Will we see the end of this one?'

'No, you will only see the middle,' said Lady Tamerlane. 'And if you don't go and get ready at once, you won't see it at all.'

In great haste we put on our outdoor things, and together with three or four nursery maids we set off for the back lodge. We did not go down the avenue but along a drive which I hadn't been on before and which wound under trees and among rhododendron bushes. It seemed a long way, and as soon as we were out of earshot of the house we got Minnie to sing to us.

Minnie knew a lot of songs, some of them modern songs about love and some of them old ballads with interesting, though somewhat mysterious, stories. These last were not unlike the stories about their sisters-in-law's cousins which the nurses told to each other when they thought we weren't listening. In a vague sort of way I imagined that Barbara Allen and the Bailiff's Daughter of Islington were relations of Minnie's, as was also the lady who ran away with the dark-eyed gypsy-o.

Charlie came home late that night,
Demanding for his lady-o,
'She is gone, she is gone,' said the old servingman,
'She is gone with the dark-eyed gypsy-o.'

I felt very sorry for Charlie and annoyed with the old servingman for being so unsympathetic, and also frightened of the gypsy-o – but then we

were all frightened of gypsies. We had read books
about children who were stolen by gypsies for
their clothes, and the Savages' nurse once knew a
little girl, I think her own sister, who was stolen
by gypsies and found in a quarry with nothing on
but her chemise. Actually the adventures that
happened to Nana Savage's relations were always
so startling that we didn't really believe any of
them, but all the same it made one uncomfortable.
Peter was particularly frightened of very old
women and would run for his life if he saw one.
He did not really like the old woman in the lodge
who came out of her dark little house to talk to us.
As he was much the most attractive of us she took
a special fancy to him and tried to make him walk
into her parlour; but he wouldn't. Although it was
not made of toffee and gingerbread the lodge did
look very like the picture of the witch's house in
Hansel and Gretel, and even the attractions of a
glass case containing a school scene, the scholars
being stuffed ferrets and the schoolmaster an owl,
could not get him beyond the porch.

The Marathon race was a long time coming.
We swung on the gate and we swung on the
chains that were stretched between white posts to
prevent carriages driving over the grass edge, and

we bickered among ourselves and we stared at the other people who had collected, and altogether we got very bored; but at last there was a murmur, 'Here they come.'

So we lined up at the side of the road and several men dressed in white trotted very slowly past. After they had gone by, another man, panting very hard, appeared. This man wore a stripy shirt which I thought prettier than the white ones and so I picked him as the winner.

'That one will win,' I said. 'I know it.'

The others looked at me to see if I had some sort of power of second sight and decided I had not.

'Then you know wrong,' said Rosamund.

Betty seemed as though she were struggling not to cry.

'But where are their golden helmets?' she asked furiously. 'Where are their shields?'

'You are a silly,' said Rosamund, 'of course people don't run races in helmets and shields.'

'But Grandmama said they would,' said Betty. 'She said so. She said they were Greek and I know what Greeks look like. I know all the pictures in Lionel's Greek history. Grandmama is an untruth-teller.'

'*Betty!*' said Rosamund, shocked. 'You mustn't say that about Grandmama.'

'She is,' said Betty. Her eyes were shiny with tears and the corners of her mouth went down.

Harry was very soft-hearted and could not bear to see Betty crying.

'As a matter of fact they did wear helmets and shields,' he said, 'only they went by so fast that they were very hard to see.'

'Did they?' asked Betty doubtfully.

'Of course they did,' he said, and appealed to the others. 'They did wear helmets and shields, didn't they? You all saw them, didn't you?'

The others were rather afraid of Betty's violent temper and agreed quickly.

'Yes, we all saw them. You must have seen them, Betty.'

Betty said that perhaps after all she had seen them. 'Sort of gold and glittering?' she suggested.

'Yes,' agreed everyone. 'Gold and glittering.'

Betty quite cheered up.

'Let's have a Marathon race of our own,' said Rosamund. 'All the way home. It must be nearly as far as from Marathon to Athens.'

'Let's! Let's!' said everyone. 'Minnie, you say "go".'

We drew up in a line with one foot stuck out so far in front that we were almost doing the splits. Minnie said: 'Are you ready, are you steady, go!' and away we went.

The Tamerlane back drive was not perhaps as far as from Marathon to Athens, but it was very long for all that. Betty, who was the smallest and fattest, dropped off first, and I, who was not used to running, soon found that I could not keep up with the others, not even with Peter. I ran as hard as I could till my head seemed bursting and my inside empty of breath, but the others went further and further ahead, and the drive was so bendy that soon they were out of sight altogether. I had meant to get great glory by winning the race, and it was disappointing to find myself puffed and tired and behind everybody except Betty.

Just when I thought I simply could not run another step I came to a small path leading off the drive. It looked like a shortcut to the house and was exactly what I wanted, and I started down it feeling rather clever, but when it stopped going straight and started winding among trees, I wondered if I had been so clever after all. The afternoon was getting late and under the trees it was very gloomy. I dropped to a walk but then remembered gypsies and started to run again. I suppose the sensible thing would have been to turn round and go back, but that never entered my head. I only thought of going faster so as to get home quicker.

To make matters worse, I came to a crossroads where five paths met, and I had no idea which one led towards the house. I chose the path which looked widest and ran on down it, by this time with a bad stitch in my side, and then to my horror I heard a horse coming along behind me.

I did not dare to look round as I was quite sure the horse was dragging a gypsy caravan, and though I tried to run faster and faster my breath was entirely gone, and the horse, though only walking, gained on me. When it was quite close to me a man's voice said:

'Hello, Atalanta!'

This was too much for me. I thought Atalanta was some magic word like Abracadabra, and with a loud scream I tried to run up a tree. I had a sort of confused idea that horses couldn't climb trees (nor caravans either) and that if I got up one I would be safe. The tree I attempted, however, had no branches anywhere near the ground, and after hugging the trunk with both arms for a second I dropped back helplessly on to the root. I lay huddled for a moment, not daring to look up, while the horse made crunchy noises and then the man's voice said:

'What on earth do you think you're doing?'

It was a kind voice, and I had heard it before. I wriggled round and looked up, seeing first the horse's muddy legs, then a very muddy boot, then some muddy white breeches, then a muddy red coat, then a face with some dried blood on it, and finally an old top hat rather crooked and a bit muddy too. I knew that gypsies didn't wear top hats, and looking more calmly I recognized the Savages' father coming back from hunting. Harry had boasted to me that his father rode 'straight' and was 'a tiger to go', and indeed he looked as if he had ridden extremely straight, through hedges, ditches, ponds, everything.

'We are having a Marathon race,' I said, as well as I could for panting. I thought he might think it rude if I told him I had mistaken him for a gypsy. 'But I seem to be lost.'

'Well, if you keep straight on you'll get to the house,' he said. 'Where's your nurse?'

'I don't have a nurse,' I said, hurt in my dignity. 'I haven't had a nurse for *years*.'

I picked myself up and began to run again. I did not want to come in behind Betty.

But the shortcut had taken me a long way round, and when I reached home there was an anxious crowd of children and nursery maids waiting by the side door. They did not dare go upstairs without me, and they did not know where to go to look for me. Harry was actually crying.

Rosamund rushed at me and seized me so violently by the arm that it hurt, and Marguerite was moved to burst into speech, but as it was all in French I don't know what she said.

'Where have you been?' everyone shouted.

I was just going to ask who had won the Marathon race when I saw that Betty was there, so it was clear that, whoever had won, it was Evelyn who had come in last.

'I decided that Marathon races are rather overdone,' I said grandly. 'So I walked home with the Savages' father. I found him a delightful man.'

Everyone was silenced by these grown-up remarks. I shook off the hands that still clutched me and, with head in air, stalked up the wooden stairs magnificently, though it is not easy to be magnificent when one is puffing and panting like a bellows.

9. The Wet Day

THE NEXT day was wet, sheets of rain pouring down so that even the Glens' nurse, who was the hardiest of the three, announced at breakfast, 'No walks. No riding.'

After breakfast we always tore off to Lady Tamerlane's room, which was at the end of a lovely, long passage with four steps up and four steps down in the middle. You can imagine the crashes as we jumped up them and then jumped down the other side. When we came to the end we used to pause to collect ourselves and to look at a picture of people on a sledge being attacked by wolves. We were frightened of wolves, even Lionel a little, but we could not help looking at the picture. Did they escape? We never knew. One could but hope for the best but fear the worst.

Then the passage zigzagged and we were in darkness as, giggling a little, we stood and knocked at Lady Tamerlane's door.

'Come in!' she always answered promptly, and we burst in and rushed to our favourite corners.

I expect you have read how in the old days when the kings of France were dressing, their rooms used to be crowded with courtiers. The scene in Lady Tamerlane's bedroom must have been rather like what the French kings put up with, except, I suppose, that courtiers would behave better than the Savages did. Lady Tamerlane was only half dressed when we came in, but at that date people wore such a lot of clothes that her petticoat had more to it than a modern person's frock. A little chest of drawers full of bead necklaces and curios was put on the floor and we chiefly played with that, while she wandered round cleaning her teeth and having her hair done by Miss Spenser, her maid.

Miss Spenser was a dear little creature with pince-nez. She looked very old and frail beside Lady Tamerlane. She brushed Lady Tamerlane's hair on and on, and then tied it in bunches with tapes, and finally pinned it up on top so cleverly that all the tapes were hidden.

Lady Tamerlane talked to us all the time, generally about the strange people she had met in the course of her life. I remember her saying that 'everyone who lives long enough knows three murderers', and then telling us about the three murderers that she had met. She had travelled a great deal and she liked talking about the countries she had visited. On this particular wet morning Harry had asked her if she had ever been in a sledge and been chased by wolves, and though she confessed she had not, she told us a story about a friend of hers who had been. That led her to tell us other stories about Russia and about Revolutionaries who threw bombs. One of her peculiarities was that she didn't bother to pronounce things properly, and 'bomb' she pronounced 'boom'.

'What's a boom, Grandmama?' asked Harry.

'She means a bomb,' said Peter, looking up from the shoes which he was arranging in a pattern.

The rest of us were shocked by this remark which we felt to be in terrible taste. Even Lady

Tamerlane looked disconcerted and quickly changed the subject.

'Everline, have you written to thank your mother and father for their presents?'

I said that I hadn't had time.

'You had better come down into my sitting room and do it this morning.'

Her hair being finished, she rose up and presented us all with Red Indian suits and there was a scrimmage as we forced ourselves into them. Most of them were a sort of khaki colour, but Betty's was green.

'I'm not a Red Indian,' said Betty. 'I'm a Green Indian.'

'There isn't such a thing,' said Rosamund. 'You've got to be a Red Indian too.'

'No, I won't,' said Betty. 'I'm a Green Indian.'

'You can't be,' said Rosamund. 'Can she, Grandmama?'

'I'm a Green Indian,' yelled Betty, flying into a rage.

'Time you all went back to the nursery,' said Lady Tamerlane, and we swept out into the passage and charged off, up the steps and down the steps, shouting, 'I'm a Red Indian!' except for Betty who shouted, 'Green Indian!'

Later on, as it was so wet, the Glens' mother and the Savages' mother also descended on their young to force them to write their thank-you letters. They had not many to write as most of their presents came from people in the house, but there were a few strays, such as godmothers, who had to be thanked. I remember that Peter had a very special godmother whom even the grown-ups seemed to hold in fear, and his mother tried to work him up into the right frame of mind to write something really showy.

'But need I write at all?' said Peter. 'She only sent me a book.'

'What was it called?' asked his mother.

'Some bosh like "The Art of Joy",' said Peter.

'It wasn't called that,' said Peggy.

'Wasn't it? Well, perhaps it was called "The Joy of Art",' said Peter carelessly. He was very bored with the whole subject.

'Where is it?' said his mother.

The book, which was called nothing about either Art or Joy, was found built into a camp for Peter's soldiers. It was very large and grand-looking, bound in imitation white vellum and its edges were gold. Gold clouds (or smoke curls) were drawn on the cover, and the pages, which were very thick with wide margins, were ornamented with the same sort of curly-wiggle. There were a few coloured pictures protected by tissue-paper, but these were also mostly of clouds (or smoke).

'What a lovely book!' exclaimed Peter's mother, stroking it respectfully.

'That sort of book is not much good really,' said Peter wisely. 'I know them of old. The pages fall out almost at once. I truly don't think it's worth thanking for.'

'You are naughty to be so ungrateful to your godmother,' put in Peggy priggishly. 'Look what lovely thick paper it is. And all those blank pages at the end! Ideal for drawing on, and you could paint on them too.'

'I'll write a letter for you and you can copy it,' said his mother. 'Your godmother will be very hurt if she doesn't get a letter.'

'All right,' said Peter amiably. 'I don't mind her sending it if she wants to. And if I paint a red cross on the lid it will make a jolly good hospital tent.'

I turned away to listen to the Savages' mother, who was having trouble with Betty. Betty's godmother had sent her a postal order for 5s. with a letter saying that she was afraid it would arrive late for Christmas. As a matter of fact it had come on Christmas Eve and Betty had got into one of her contrary moods and said that she wouldn't accept it.

'If I write a letter, will you put "Love from Betty" at the bottom?' said her mother.

'No,' said Betty. 'I'll put "Hate from Betty".'

'It's no good,' said Harry. 'Nothing will make her change her mind now. But I'll write "Love from Betty" all blotchy and her godmother won't know the difference.'

'If you do,' said Betty, 'I'll throw your bedroom slippers into the fire.'

She would have, too. I did not wait to see the end of this discussion but went mincing off to Lady Tamerlane's sitting room. I was still dressed in my Red Indian clothes, and the feathers on my head and the beads and bobbles made me feel particularly elegant and grown-up.

I found Lady Tamerlane in the Chinese Room writing away at her own letters. There was another writing table, however, and she told me to sit down at it and to start. I was annoyed that she was occupied with her own affairs as I hoped that she would let me spend the whole morning with her, away from the nursery, and being too stupid to realize that busy people don't like being interrupted by even the most intelligent child, I thought it a wonderful opportunity for making friends with her. I remembered acrostics and the Italian poetry, and not having any idea what an acrostic was I said:

'Shall I write to Mamma in Italian?'

Lady Tamerlane looked up in surprise and said:

'Do you know Italian?'

'No.'

'Then write in English.'

She began scribbling away again, but I was determined to be noticed.

'I think this nib is bent,' I said.

'Use a pencil.'

There were two pencils there, both beautifully sharpened by Mr O'Sullivan. I looked round for other ways of making myself noticed. My eyes fell on a pot plant.

'Oh, Lady Tamerlane, what is the name of that lovely flower?'

Lady Tamerlane knew nothing about flowers and cared less.

'Write what you've got to, first,' she said, 'you may talk afterwards.'

There was nothing else for it. I had to get on with my letter. The pen, of course, was perfectly all right, but I was not used to writing in ink and I kept dipping too far into the silver inkpot (which was filled exactly to the brim) and making terrible blots. My fingers got covered with ink and the blotting-paper and my face became very messy, and I was not helped by the tags and feathers on my Red Indian suit. I could not see into the ballroom as curtains had been let down across the alcove, but the Chinese Room was full of small attractive objects and I kept looking about me instead of getting on with what I was supposed to be doing.

At last, however, I did get some sort of letter finished and I brought it over to Lady Tamerlane, who looked at it without surprise, though equally without admiration. She put it into an envelope which she had already addressed for me and then tossed it into a tray on top of her own letters. The never-failing Mr O'Sullivan would remove them, stamp them and see that they caught the next post.

Lady Tamerlane at once began writing again, but I tried to linger.

'Shall I arrange your papers for you?' I asked.

'Run along, Everline,' said Lady Tamerlane, not even thanking me for my kind offer, and with unwilling feet I left the realm of faery and went back to the nursery wing.

There I found the other children rather inky but still partially dressed as Red Indians. They were sitting in the passage playing grandmother's garden-party, a game of which they were very fond. It began:

'My grandmother gave a garden party and invited Pincher.'

'My grandmother gave a garden party and invited Pincher and Charles I.'

'My grandmother gave a garden party and invited Pincher, Charles I and Tommy Howliboo.' And so on.

One might have thought it was a peaceful sort of game, but presently the list included 'Lionel and the King of the Donkeys . . .', and Harry *would* say, 'Lionel-the-King-of-the-Donkeys'. Lionel threw himself on top of Harry and there was a fight in which everybody joined, and which only ended when Harry's head bumped a door handle and broke it in half. We cooled down at once and looked at the two pieces in dismay.

'Let's say you slipped up and bumped against the handle by mistake,' said Rosamund.

We agreed to this sensible suggestion and we sat down again and began asking each other riddles and catches. Most of them were designed to make the person say that they were a donkey. Rosamund produced a new one which none of us had heard before. 'What is the difference between a piano, a cigar and your face?' The answer was, 'A piano makes music, a cigar makes you sick, and your face makes me sick'. Rosamund knew a lot of riddles. I never could discover where she got them from. Perhaps she made them up. Somebody has to.

The passage we were sitting in had nothing much in it except some fire extinguishers and some hot-water pipes running along the skirting which we kept trying to perch on, not very successfully, as they were too narrow and too hot. For want of anything better to do, we began examining the extinguishers. They were of two sorts – fat blue bottles about the size of croquet balls, which I think you were supposed to hurl into the flames like grenades, and tall red metal cans. It was obvious that we could not break one of the blue bottles without being found out, but

Lionel, after reading the directions on one of the red tins, said:

'I wonder if this is in working order. I think we ought to test it. Very dangerous having fire extinguishers that don't work. Most unwise. Extremely rash.'

We crowded round.

'The way that this particular breed of extinguisher operates,' said Lionel, looking again at the directions, 'is to point the nozzle of the hose at the appropriate object and then with the hammer strike a smart blow on mark "A".'

He unwound the hose and took the little gold hammer out of its socket.

'Don't do it!' 'Do do it!' we clamoured.

'If the nozzle is pointed out of the window, the apparatus can be tested in perfect safety,' said Lionel grandly.

Peter said that he thought he heard Grandpapa's bath chair being pushed under the window and we craned our necks out to look: but it was much too wet for anyone, even a gardener, to be about. Immediately below the window there were nothing but laurel bushes and ivy and an ancient seat under an iron trellis.

'It's only the ivy bower below,' said Lionel. '*That* doesn't matter. I won't squirt much, only a little to see if it is in good order.'

Rosamund told us afterwards that she meant to ask him if he knew how to turn the thing off, but she forgot to say it. Instead she remarked, 'I wonder if we oughtn't to test *all* the extinguishers all over the house.'

Peggy was Lionel's favourite for the time being, and he gave her the nozzle to point out of the window. She held it at arm's length while Lionel raised the hammer.

'Stand back and watch the effect,' he said, and struck a smart blow with the hammer on mark 'A'.

Nothing happened. Lionel hit it again. Nothing.

'I'm deeply afraid it's empty,' said Harry.

Lionel shook the thing and we could hear the water slopping about inside.

'And it won't be water,' said Lionel, 'it will be some sort of deadly poison. It's an infernal machine.'

Peggy held the nozzle still further away from her face.

'Simply bash it,' said Rosamund. 'Take a run at it. One, two, three, *bash*!'

Lionel retreated to a distance and then rushed forward and with the gold hammer hit mark 'A' as hard as he could. There was a loud squish-hiss and Lionel sprang back even faster than he came, for the infernal machine began in a gush, not, unfortunately, from the nozzle, but from where the hose joined the tin. We had failed to notice that the rubber at the joint had perished.

Deadly poison squirted in all directions (except out of the window).

'Help!' we screamed, leaping up and down, 'Flood! Fire! Plague! Pestilence! Famine!'

Nana Glen appeared, took one look and sent her nursery maid running off for Mr O'Sullivan, and we capered about yelling while the extinguisher continued to play like a fountain.

'Will it go on for ever?' asked Peter, rather appalled.

'Yes it will,' cried Rosamund. 'It's like the burning bush, only water.'

In another moment Mr O'Sullivan had appeared among us, looking even taller than usual in his shirtsleeves, and without stopping to ask silly questions he had picked up the fountain and heaved it out of the window. We heard it crash on to the ivy bower below, and peering out we could see it continuing to play, spraying the lovers' seat with poison.

'Ho, ho, and who did that?' asked Mr O'Sullivan, looking from the drenched passage to the row of frightened but exhilarated children.

'Lionel!' we cried. 'Lionel did it!' Lionel was never punished, not even put into disgrace, so we had no compunction about giving him away.

'You all helped,' said Lionel unsportingly.

Peggy said in a very gentle voice, 'I don't see why Grandmama need be told.'

Everyone saw the point of that, and the nursery maid was sent to see if the wet had soaked through into the passage below, and when she came back and reported that it had not, we surrounded Mr O'Sullivan.

'Oh, please don't tell Grandmama, Mr O'Sullivan. Please don't tell.'

Mr O'Sullivan looked solemn, so very solemn that we knew he was going to help.

'Get one of your girls to mop up the passage,' he said to Nana Glen, 'and I'll move the bag of tricks out of the cosy corner before anyone sees it.'

'Oh, thank you,' we cried. 'Thank you! Thank you!'

Mr O'Sullivan said nothing more, but he stooped and picked up one of the blue glass extinguishers and made pretence to throw it at Lionel's head. Lionel ducked in terror, and Mr O'Sullivan put the bottle back in its wire holder and disappeared down the back stairs, chuckling to himself.

'You'd better all come along into the nursery,' said Nana Glen, adding, 'though I'm sure we don't want Lionel.'

'The same to you with knobs on,' retorted Lionel. 'I shall go down to Mamma.'

'May I come with you?' I asked daringly.

Lionel looked annoyed, but said, 'All right,' so we set off together, Lionel talking at a great rate. He told me about battles and killings, but whether he was telling me about the Ancient Greeks or about the history of his own imaginary country, I had no idea. Not that I cared anyway. I wasn't listening. What I enjoyed was leaving the other children behind and going off with a big boy like Lionel.

Downstairs we wandered about from room to room. At every writing table there was a grown-up writing letters who glanced at us as we came by and then looked away again. At last one of the letter-writers turned out to be Lionel's mother. She laid down her pen and stroked his hair and said:

'Anything wrong in the nursery?'

'Yes, there is,' said Lionel in a loud, complaining voice. 'They've all got this insane craze for persecution. There's been nothing like it since the Early Christians.'

'What have they been doing?' asked his mother with anxiety.

Lionel looked sideways at me and then said cautiously:

'A deed without a name.'

'Oh dear,' said his mother, and I could see that she was longing to get back to her letter. 'Could you and Evelyn play a game together?'

'No,' said Lionel. 'But if you gave us some writing paper we could draw pictures.'

Every child knows that drawing pictures on the writing paper is against the rules, but Lionel's mother, after a glance round to see that no one was looking, handed us each a sheet.

'Black-edged, please,' said Lionel. 'It makes a sort of frame.'

On all the writing tables in the house there were a few sheets of black-edged paper in case any of the visitors should be in mourning. So we each got a black-edged sheet and a magazine to prop it on and a pencil with a beautiful smooth point, and we settled ourselves down to draw.

The only things I knew how to draw were fairies, so I drew the fairy queen with fairies all round her.

Lionel finished first and showed his picture to his mother.

'Whatever is it meant to be?' she said. 'It looks like some sort of fountain, only why is everyone running away from it?'

Lionel showed it to me.

'Do you know what it is, Evelyn?'

I knew perfectly well, but I didn't dare say. I shook my head and said, 'I think you have drawn it beautifully, Lionel. I wish I could draw as well as you do.'

'Well, as none of you seem able to guess,' said Lionel, 'I'll tell you what it is. It is a very dangerous sort of fountain which spurts deadly poison.'

'Really!' said his mother. 'It doesn't sound at all a safe sort of thing to have about.'

'It isn't,' said Lionel.

'Perhaps someone will throw it out of the window,' I suggested.

'Almost certainly they will,' said Lionel. He suddenly decided to like me. 'When it stops raining I will show you my Secret Place,' he said.

I fully understood that this was a very great honour and I thanked him profusely. All through dinner I looked forward to going off with Lionel and leaving the other children behind, but to my disappointment the rain continued to come down as hard as ever, and we had to think of something to do indoors. What with the babies and what with the nurses, there really was not room for us in the nursery, so out we came into the passages again, still wearing our Indian headdresses, and played hide-and-seek. We were told not to go into any of the bedrooms nor downstairs, but there were so many passages that we got along very well and enjoyed ourselves with the exception of Betty, who took all games in deadly earnest and was as frightened as if she were being chased by real Indians. Peter, too, was troubled and anxious as he had been told the story of the lady who hid in a chest and then couldn't open the lid, and hundreds of years later they found her skeleton. The only chests in the passages were chests of drawers which he could not possibly have shut himself into, but he was worried all the same.

Just when hide-and-seek was beginning to pall, Rosamund appeared with a finger on her lip, and such an important expression on her face that we saw at once that she had made an exciting discovery. She held up her other hand for silence and said impressively:

'We are in luck. The key is in the door of the lumber room. Come, braves and squaws, and attack the wigwams of the enemy.'

Till that moment I had never heard of the lumber room, but I joined in the rush with the rest. Sure enough, the key was in the lock, and Rosamund, who had made the discovery, was allowed to turn it, and open the door and walk in first. We pushed in behind her.

As soon as we got inside it became perfectly clear why the door was generally kept locked. In the middle of the floor was a glass dome, looking rather like a small greenhouse, which acted as a skylight to the billiard room which was just below. Suppose a child were to fall, or be pushed, against the glass, he would probably fall through it, down into the billiard room.

'I wonder what Aunt Muriel's Husband would say if Betty came hurtling through the skylight just when he was in the middle of a stroke,' said Harry.

'Is he there now?' said Betty, trying to squint through one of the little stars in the frosted glass.

We all leant against the glass trying to look through, but it fortunately supported us. Some of us thought we could see everything in the room below, including all the uncles playing billiards: others confessed that they could see nothing whatever.

The lumber room was full of things such as birdcages and tin baths and also old furniture, some of it broken and shabby and all of it dusty. Many of the pieces would nowadays be considered extremely smart, but in those days they were out of fashion. However, Chippendale or Regency meant nothing to us, and we clambered about happily, pretending we were in a forest tracking palefaces, until Rosamund, always adventurous, pointed to a ladder and said 'Excelsior!'

The rest of us turned round and looked. On either side, high up in the wall, were two doors leading into that gap between ceiling and roof that there sometimes is in houses. A plank stretched from one to the other. It was high above our heads and went over the glass dome which, as you remember, was in the middle of the room. The ladder rested on the plank, and by going up it you could obviously get through one of the doors and explore the garret.

Giggling and nervous we followed each other up the ladder. There was an awkward place at the top where we had to get off the ladder and on to the plank, but we all managed it, even Betty, who was so anxious not to be left behind and to show that she was as good as any of us and better, that she nearly shot right over it.

The garret was very dark except near the doorway. There were beams across the floor rather like railway sleepers and if you missed one and your foot slipped down between them, there was a crackle of breaking plaster.

'Don't do that, Peter,' said Peggy severely, as Peter fell off his beam for the second time. 'You will go right through and Grandmama will be puce if she looks up and sees your foot sticking through her bedroom ceiling.'

'I don't believe Grandmama's bedroom is underneath,' said Peter, 'and anyway she wouldn't be sitting in her bedroom in the middle of the afternoon.'

'She might have gone to fetch something,' said Harry, who was always ready for an argument. 'Bother!' He bumped into a beam which barred his way and fell on to the plaster with both feet. 'Oh, don't leave me behind.'

'Forwards!' cried Lionel, who had got well ahead and was never one to wait for stragglers. 'Follow the trail. Death to the palefaces.'

For a time we stumbled along in the dark, climbing over and under the supports of the roof, until we were tired of it. The little ones at the back got very behind and called, 'Wait! Oh, do wait!' without any effect, but at last there was a glimmer of light and a halt.

I caught up with Lionel and Rosamund and found that they had stopped under a skylight and there was another skylight in the floor. We got on our hands and knees round it and peered down on to a strip of passage that at first seemed so strange and entrancing that we wanted to jump down to it at once. But Betty recognized a washing hamper and we realized that we were only looking down on to the familiar passage outside the nursery maids' bedrooms. Harry brought out of his pocket a lot of tiny sandbags belonging to his toy soldiers.

'Let's drop them on people's heads,' he said. One of the panes of glass was open and we piled the ammunition round it. As soon as we heard footsteps we tipped them over without waiting to see who was below.

'Crumbs! It's Nana!' said Peter.

For a moment Nana Glen stood below speechlessly, staring up at us, sandbags all round her on the floor. Speechlessly we stared down on her. Then, without exchanging a word, she turned and was off.

'She's gone to fetch Grandmama!'

In fearful haste we left the skylight and plunged into the darkness again.

'Not so fast! Don't leave me behind!' wailed the little ones, falling on to the plaster at almost every step.

'Come on,' said the big ones angrily. 'Let's get down the ladder before anyone comes.'

But when we got to the crack of light that showed that our tour was at an end and that we had reached the other door, there was a stop. The big ones fumbled but could find no handle. The little ones came up and asked:

'What is it?'

'Actually, it's fastened by a hook on the outside,' remarked Harry. 'I remember noticing it as I was coming up the ladder.'

'Then why on earth didn't you say so before?' asked Rosamund crossly (and she had some reason to be cross).

'I thought everyone knew,' said Harry.

We stood in a huddle and rattled the door.

'Hist!' said Rosamund, who thought that an unusual situation needed unusual language, 'one cometh up the ladder.'

We kept quiet and listened, and we could certainly hear a person getting off the ladder and coming across the plank. Then the door was unlatched and the light streamed in, and to our thankfulness the face that we beheld was that of Mr O'Sullivan. We welcomed him with enthusiasm.

'Now you've done it,' he said with a wink.

We then perceived that he was not alone. Below, standing among the dusty lumber, was the Savages' mother. She was a very nervous lady, and when she was frightened she became very angry (as most of us do). She looked up at us with a white, grim face.

Lionel advanced upon the plank.

'What are you doing up there?' said his mother through clenched teeth.

'I'll give you twenty questions and three guesses,' said Lionel who, as you may have noticed, was very spoilt. He wobbled slightly.

'Well, come down at once,' said his mother in a strangled voice.

'Am I to be punished?'

'Come down.'

'Not till you tell me whether I'm to be punished.'

'Oh, do come down.'

Lionel saw he was winning. It was pure showing-off anyway, as he never was punished.

'There are three things I might do. A, I might stay where I am. B, I might go back into the roof. C, I might dive through the glass into the billiard room.' He put his hands above his head as though preparing to dive.

'Don't stand there blathering. Come down.'

'Promise I'm not to be punished or even put into disgrace.'

'And the rest of us, too,' prompted Rosamund.

'And the rest of them, too,' said Lionel. 'Otherwise I'm afraid it's ye olde billiard room for me.'

'Anything you like,' said his mother desperately.

One by one we walked across the dreadful plank, a very draggled tribe of Indians. Mr O'Sullivan helped us to get on to the ladder, but even so, my knees were shaking so much that I could only just manage it. One by one we filed past the Savages' mother.

When we were all out of the lumber room Mr O'Sullivan locked the door and put the key into his pocket.

The only one of us who was not in the least ashamed was Lionel.

'I want you to read to me,' he said calmly to his mother and went off with her.

The rest of us trooped silently to the nursery, sure of a scolding for having got so dirty and only cheered by a glimpse of Mr O'Sullivan disappearing into the back regions with the lumber-room key balanced on the end of his nose.

10. Lionel's Play

NEXT day Lionel did indeed show me his Secret Place, which was in a hut in the wood which the children called the Little Trespassing House. It had a broken window-catch so that it was quite easy to get into it.

I admired it profusely, although there was nothing much to admire except sacks of pheasant food; however, Lionel lifted up an empty sack and revealed some Christmas cards which he and Peggy had removed from different mantelpieces, and also a jar half full of bull's-eyes.

We sat on the sacks and ate the bull's-eyes, and Lionel talked and I agreed with everything he said, sometimes before he had said it. Lionel liked my admiration. He talked faster and faster, until at last he suddenly stopped and said:

'I think I'll make you Berengaria.'

'How *lovely*!' I said at once. 'Make me what?'

'Berengaria. She's the heroine of my play.'

'But I thought Peggy was to be heroine.'

'She was,' said Lionel carelessly. 'But I've changed my mind. Let's go and tell Mamma. She may have to alter the clothes.'

We found his mother writing letters as usual, and he explained about Berengaria.

'But won't Peggy be very disappointed?'

'Oh, I can easily write another part for her,' said Lionel. 'She can be one of the revellers-and-attendants and a captive maiden. And she can be killed in the battle at the end. We really do need more people to be the enemy. It should look as if I was fighting against overwhelming odds. Peggy will have three parts which will be better than just one. She ought to be pleased. So alter the clothes to fit Evelyn.'

'Well, break it gently to Peggy,' said his mother. 'Perhaps I'd better come with you and help you to put it tactfully.'

After looking about the garden we found Peggy outside the potting shed giving sugar to the garden horse, Major. Major mowed the lawns in the summer, and in the winter pulled a cart about. He wore leather overshoes fastened on with straps and buckles, as Lord Tamerlane could not bear hoof-marks on the paths and, although past noticing anything very much, he could still detect a hoof-mark, however faint.

'You're not to be Berengaria,' said Lionel abruptly without waiting for his mother to lead delicately up to the subject. 'Evelyn's to be it.'

'But you are to have three other parts,' Lionel's mother hastened to put in, 'and three changes of tunic.'

I expected to see Peggy go red and possibly cry, but she only said, 'I'm glad. Berengaria had to say such awful things. Need I be in the play at all?'

'Don't you want to be?' asked Lionel, appalled.

'No,' said Peggy. '(Dear old Major, good old Major. Don't snatch, good boy.) It's all so silly.' She began to talk to the horse again, and we three slunk away feeling small.

'*I* don't think your play silly,' I said to Lionel as we went back to the house.

'It's Peggy who's silly,' said Lionel crossly.

I strutted along feeling that success had come to me at last, and when I was shown the dress that Berengaria would wear, I was more pleased than ever that I was to be the heroine. The dress was pale blue with little gold stars on it and there was also a pink satin cloak which had once belonged to one of the aunts, and a gold paper crown and a spangled veil. I was much the same size as Peggy and the things fitted me without having to be altered. I also saw the piles of cloaks and tunics that had been got ready for the other children. They were mostly made of a shiny stuff called sateen, which sounded very grand and was very cheap. Lionel's own cloak was a green velvet one, the pick of the acting box, always worn by the hero of every play.

'You'd better learn your part,' said Lionel, offering me a small washing book. I opened it and read:

'6 bath-towels, 3 pillowslips . . .'

'Further on, idiot,' said Lionel.

I turned the pages and came to a lot of very faint pencil writing. 'The Dragons' was written quite clearly at the top and there was a picture of two dragons on their hind legs, but apart from that I couldn't make out any of it. Each page was rather more scrawly than the one before, except the last which was suddenly legible as Lionel had written in block letters, 'HERE AMIDST THE LOUD APPLAUSE OF THE AUDIENCE THE PLAY ENDS'.

'I'm afraid I can't read it, Lionel.'

Lionel snatched it from me, but after puzzling over it he had to admit that it was beyond him also.

'But it doesn't matter,' he said, 'I can make my part up as I go along, and you don't have to say much anyway. It's chiefly "Alas!" and "Woe!" and that sort of thing, and "Must I then die?" when they burn you at the stake.'

'Do I really get burnt?'

'No, I rescue you, but your toes have been burnt off so that you walk with a limp for the rest of your life.'

We had several rehearsals of the play. They took place in the drawing room, a room in which the gilt furniture was so stiff and forbidding that no one usually went into it. We must have been a very tiresome team of actors as the little ones had no idea what the play was supposed to be about, and they giggled and talked and stood on one leg and forgot when they were supposed to come on. Lionel used to get frantic and wave his arms and pull his own hair.

I was the only person who really tried, and I was trying my very hardest as I was so pleased to be heroine. I was looking forward to wearing the gorgeous clothes and I had a sort of feeling that I had a real gift for acting. Perhaps, I thought, I was what I had heard my governess describe as a 'heaven-sent actress'. Perhaps the house party would be stunned by my beautiful appearance and overwhelmed by the pathos of my voice. Perhaps they would recognize me as a genius.

I could not quite imagine myself stunning Lady Tamerlane, or even the aunts, let alone the uncles, but I thought that among the audience there might be someone I had not noticed before. Perhaps that person would rise up and say, 'This child is a genius. Let me take her away and train her and she will become a great actress. Indeed, she *is* a great actress now.'

I was often so busy thinking of this sort of thing that I forgot to come in at the right place, and Lionel's mother who was rehearsing us used to say, 'Evelyn! Evelyn! Do pay attention.'

Actually it was not easy to recognize one's cues as Lionel used to make his part up as he went along and only stop when his imagination ran out, and sometimes the things that I was supposed to say didn't fit at all. However, it never seemed to matter very much, and the two big cousins, Malcolm and Alister, were very much worse than I was. Malcolm had been honoured with the part of the villain, Abun, but he had been roped in against his will and he thought the whole thing beneath his dignity and was not helpful at all.

When no one could stand any more rehearsals the play was acted in the library which, as I have said, was a very long room. Half of it was filled with chairs, and when all the visitors and servants were seated, there were supposed to be sixty people there. I don't know who counted them, but we all agreed that we were performing in front of sixty people.

There was a window at one end and curtains were pulled across this, and we acted in front of the curtains. At the sides were screens for us to lurk behind.

Dressing us took a very long time. We put our fancy dresses over our ordinary clothes and our evening shoes stuck out at the bottom. The tunics had been made with very small holes for our heads, so each one had to be wrenched down by a grown-up. Of course that made the girls' hair very untidy, and someone had to go and get all our hairbrushes down from our bedrooms.

Harry and Betty had the most amusing clothes as they were the Dragons. One wore a cardboard bulldog's head, the other a bear's. They had green tunics and green stockings and green gloves (white cotton ones dyed), and they wore bedroom slippers under their stockings in case they trod on a tintack. Their tails were long green bags fastened to their backs and stuffed with newspapers.

At last we were supposed to be ready, and the play started by Alister Glen giving the audience a tune on Nana Glen's gramophone. Gramophones were a fairly new invention, and records, instead of being flat, were round like bits of drainpipe. Each one lived in a dear little box of its own, but they were a nuisance to carry about, and Alister had only brought down one to the library. It was called 'The Galloping Major' and I thought it was something to do with the garden pony. I could not understand it anyway, although Alister played it very slowly. It turned out that we were not really ready after all, and Alister had to play it four times before Lionel, green velvet cloak and all, walked in front of the curtains, held up his hand for silence, and announced 'The Dragons'.

Lady Tamerlane clapped and everyone else did too. Lionel went out again and there was another long pause broken only by Tommy Howliboo saying in his piercing child's voice, 'Is it over? Can I go away now?'

I got behind one of the screens in a place from where I could see the audience. Lady Tamerlane was sitting in front with the aunts. Howliboos and the Savage baby were held on laps. Fathers and uncles were at the side, and there were quantities of servants behind. There were such a lot of people that they all looked rather a blur, and hidden away among the crowd might easily have been the stranger who was going to recognize me as a genius.

At last Lionel came on again and walked up and down in a most natural manner, exactly as he did in real life when something had annoyed him.

'I'm in love! I'm in love!' he said. 'Oh, what a bore! Oh, what a bore!'

That was the signal for Malcolm Glen, alias Abun, to knock on the shutters and poke his head between the curtains. He knocked on the shutters with such force that the burglar bell that was fixed to them started to ring, and when his head appeared he made faces, squinting first outwards and then cross-eyed, so that everyone began to laugh.

Lionel waited, frowning, till the burglar bell ceased jangling and then said:

'Who art thou?'

'I am a bun,' replied Abun.

'Wretch, villain, traitor,' shouted Lionel with real fury.

The whole play was less tragic than Lionel had intended. When it was my turn to enter I came in sideways, carefully facing the audience as I had been told to do, and incidentally looking out for my unknown admirer. But I quite forgot to look at Lionel who was proposing to me, as I was thinking of my crown and my veil and my pink cloak and my blue dress with the gold stars, and I was trying to see my reflection in the glass of one of the pictures.

'Wilt thou be mine?' asked Lionel.

'Alas! I am betrothed to Malcolm, I mean a bun,' I replied, smiling at Mr O'Sullivan whose eye I had just caught.

'Do pay attention, Berengaria,' said poor Lionel, but he could say no more, for at that moment he was attacked by violent hiccoughs.

'Dost thou love me?' I asked him.

'Hic!' answered Lionel.

'Wilt thou show thy love by slaying my betrothed?'

'Hic!'

Mr O'Sullivan now came out of the audience with a glass of water which Lionel drank, and the hiccoughs stopped enough for him to hiss 'Dragons! Dragons! Come on, Dragons!'

The whisper came back:

'Betty says her nose is bleeding.'

'Stuff in a handkerchief and send her on *instanter.*'

Rosamund stuffed a handkerchief up the neck of the bulldog and the Dragons scuttled in on hands and knees.

Harry said afterwards that he couldn't see as his mask had slipped, and Betty said that she could see Harry's tail through one eye-hole and followed that. At any rate, they passed the hero and heroine at full tilt and rushed straight to the front row of the audience where they sat up and begged.

'Capital! Capital!' said Lady Tamerlane.

They really looked rather horrifying, specially the little green paws, and Tommy Howliboo burst into tears. The girl Howliboo was much braver and gave the bear a smart smack on the nose.

'Dragons to heel!' cried Lionel despairingly.

I don't think any author can ever have had such tiresome performers. Even Rosamund let him down. She had to bring on some magic sandals and say, 'Here are the sandals of Horsa,' and instead she said, 'Here are the handles of saucer,' and then stopped and giggled. But nobody annoyed him so much as I did when we came to the part where I was to be burnt at the stake.

Some logs of wood were brought in from the basket in the hall and were piled round a fire-screen, the sort that is on a pole. I sat down as gracefully as I could on top of the logs and Peter tied me to the pole with a flimsy piece of string. Peter was not good at tying knots and he couldn't get it to stay fastened.

'Crumbs!' he said at last and gave it up.

For once Lionel was not on the stage, and I was entirely the centre of interest and I felt entirely pleased with myself. My pink satin cloak billowed around me, and I pointed one of my bronze shoes elegantly and smiled sweetly on everyone.

Alister came up with a box of Bryant & May's safety matches, and I tossed back my hair and smiled at him also. Alister struck a match, blew it out, pretended to light the logs with it, and said cheerfully:

'See the flames leap round her. Now her feet are gone. Soon she will be a heap of ashes.'

From behind the screen came Lionel's voice:

'Stop smiling or I'll kill you.'

The final scene was the grand battle which Lionel had to win against overwhelming odds. I stood waving a handkerchief on a chair, supposed to be a tower, from which I had a good view of the battlefield.

The first to fall was Peggy who, having in the course of the evening been pulled in and out of three tunics to show that she was three separate people, ran on looking extremely tousled, and collapsed thankfully under the bagatelle table. Betty was driven into the audience by Alister. He got her by the foot and she, yelling blue murder and quite forgetting that it was only a play, hung on to the chair on which her father was sitting.

Lionel was chased round and round by Abun waving a cardboard sword, but when all seemed lost Abun remembered that it was his duty to die and so, after giving Lionel one final stab, lay down flat on his back with his eyes shut.

'So perish all traitors,' said Lionel, turning hastily round and putting his foot on the corpse of his enemy. 'Berengaria! My own!'

But at this point the heroine, craning her neck in one last long look for her admirer in the audience, overbalanced and fell off the chair on top of the remaining Dragon who was mauling Peter.

'Oh, you *fool*!' cried the hero.

After it was over everyone crowded round Lionel to congratulate him. I, thoroughly pleased with myself, came up with the others, expecting compliments as I felt I had performed very gracefully and remembered a good deal of my part, even if not all. But Lionel was extremely angry.

'Smiling when you're being burnt at the stake!' he said, kicking a gilt chair. '*Smiling*! But I'll tell you what I'll do. Next year I'll write a play that will be something like a play. There will be a hero who will be me of course, and there *won't be a heroine at all*. So there.'

11. The Grotto

THE NEXT day Lionel was still angry with me. He refused to answer my well-meant remarks and became very affable to his own family. He even spoke to Betty, a thing I had never seen him do before.

The whole Savage family (except the baby) had become suddenly possessed with the idea that they must write a magazine. I expect actually it was Lionel who started the idea – he generally did start their ideas – but they all became keen on it and said 'magazine' over and over again as though it were some sort of password. Betty didn't know what a magazine was, but that didn't stop her from talking about it.

After breakfast the Savages all lay down on their fronts in a corner of the nursery and began to write. Betty could not write but she drew picture puzzles. The Glens, who did not like writing, went down to the still room to talk to Mrs Peabody.

I sauntered over to the group of Savages and stood beside them. None of them raised their heads.

'Shall I write something for your magazine?' I asked.

'No,' said Lionel, scribbling away hard. 'This is going to be a very unusual magazine and all the stories admitted to it are going to be good.'

'But I'd write a good story.'

'You couldn't.'

I returned sadly to the hearthrug where Tommy Howliboo was beating on an old tin with a stick.

'Why are you doing that, Tommy?'

'To keep away dwagons. Too many dwagons here.'

'Were you frightened of the dragons last night?'

'Course not. Me were only joking.'

He was a dear little boy when he was not frightened and I played with him for a bit, but I could not forget those older, bigger, more important children at the other end of the nursery, and I soon left him and went back to hover round the Savages. They still did not look up, but they made no objection to my reading the loose sheets of paper that were lying about on the floor; in fact Harry pushed a poem towards me with his foot. It was very short and went (I leave the spelling to your imagination):

> *Oh listen all ye Savages,*
> *About to choose a bride.*
> *Don't choose a one with asthma*
> *And don't choose a one that's died.*

Rosamund was writing a story called 'Nora's Adventure'. It was about a girl who was sent to school to improve her, and she got into the train at a small station in the north of Scotland. 'She sat sadly without looking up for a few minutes but as the whistle sounded something flashing in at the window attracted her attention. It was a splendid golden eagle. He caught Nora in his beak as the train began to move. Now although Nora was tall she was thin and light and so the eagle carried her quite easily. There was a strong wind blowing so neither the stationmaster nor the porter in the little Highland station heard her cries . . .'

'I'm sure the porter would have noticed,' I said, wishing to find fault.

'He might have on an ordinary day,' said Rosamund, 'but I've specially told you that a strong wind was blowing.'

'And also, if you said that Nora was small for her age it would be better.'

But Rosamund could not bring herself to make her heroine small for her age.

'No, it wouldn't. I've said she was thin and light and that's quite enough.'

I shrugged my shoulders, which was a gesture I was very fond of. I thought it grown-up but the Savages called it affected.

Lionel wrote so quickly that he had already covered many pages. His story was about school life and was called 'What happened to boys who committed murder and other bad things don't take their example'. In the preface he explained that 'the habits of the school are much like those of the school I am at', and as I had never been to school myself I read with interest to see what it was really like. Lionel's writing was terribly difficult, but as far as I could make out, school was a very tough place indeed. For instance, in the chapter called 'Trinity Sunday' they were all in the school chapel when there was a smashing of glass and a spear came flying through the window. 'It hit Ritard. With a cry he rose and walked out of the pew and fell dead in the aisle. The captain of the school carried him out and the service went on as if nothing had happened . . .'

Lionel, I knew, was not happy at school and really I was not at all surprised.

Writing stories looked so easy that I got some paper by tearing the flyleaves out of several books. To find a pencil with a point was harder, but fortunately I had had a diary in my stocking, so I took the pencil out of that and was soon scribbling away as fast as the others.

My story was about some children who had a shell grotto in their garden, and they dug up the floor of it and found some buried treasure underneath. So then they were immensely rich, much richer than any of the grown-ups, and they never had to do a thing they didn't like ever again. The buried treasure had been put there by smugglers, and that part I copycatted from a story about smugglers that was in a *Chatterbox Annual* which I had got for Christmas. *Chatterbox* had been kept in my bedroom and no one had read it except myself, so I knew that the others would not be able to catch me out.

But the others wouldn't even look at my story.

'We really don't want it, Evelyn,' said Rosamund, as kindly as she could, after whispering to Lionel, who said, not at all kindly:

'Take the bally thing away.'

I was disappointed and hurt. To make things worse, when the time came for me to go out for our morning walk I was slow getting ready and when I arrived downstairs I found that everyone was paired off and no one seemed to want me as a third, so that I felt more left out of it than ever.

I walked along the muddy road beside Marguerite who, as usual, was totally silent, and I brooded over my wrongs and over the beautiful buried treasure in the grotto which I had taken the trouble to invent but in which no one would take any interest.

I brooded all through rest and all through dinner, and after dinner when we were turned out into the garden, I said:

'Don't count me in the eena-meena. I'm not going to play. I'm going to see if I can't find this buried treasure.'

'What buried treasure?' asked Rosamund, falling into the trap.

'The buried treasure your grandmother was talking about,' I said.

'When was she talking about buried treasure?' asked Rosamund.

'I think I did hear her say something about buried treasure,' said Harry, unexpectedly coming to my help. Harry was so given to romancing himself that he really didn't know the difference between what really happened and what was just make-up. 'I wasn't supposed to be listening, but I do remember her saying, "Sure as eggs is eggs there's a blinking great packet."'

'I'm sure Grandmama never said anything of the sort,' said Rosamund. 'You've been reading something.'

'Didn't she?' said Harry. 'Oh, well, I remember now, what she said was, "The lucky beggar who finds it will get a tidy-sized 'oard."'

'Well, where did she say it was?' asked everybody.

'It was,' said Harry slowly, looking up at the sky. 'Let me see . . .' His eyes wandered round searching for a likely place.

'I thought she said it was buried in the grotto,' I suggested softly.

'Yes,' said Harry. 'Grandmama, when she buried her buried treasure, did bury it in the grotto.'

'But that's ridiculous,' said Peggy, who was much the most sensible of the lot – in fact I might say the only sensible one of the lot, 'Grandmama wouldn't bury treasure. She can't dig for one thing.'

'Harry's got it a little wrong,' I said, 'the buried treasure has been in the grotto for ages and ages, only no one dares to dig it up because of the roof not being safe, and people only going into it occasionally.'

'But who put it there?' asked Peggy.

'Smugglers,' I replied at once.

'But there couldn't have been smugglers here. We're miles from the seaside,' said Lionel.

'That's why they came, of course,' I said. 'It was a safe place. The coastguards would look everywhere at the seaside but they wouldn't think of looking here.'

'True,' said Rosamund.

I could see that they were interested and, certain that none of them had read my *Chatterbox*, I went on, 'They were called the Nightriders because they rode by night. They had to get the treasure to London and, if you come to think of it, we are plumb in the way between London and the sea.'

After I had said this I wondered if I was right, but to my relief the older ones, who knew a little geography, agreed that this was so.

'Let's go and dig it up,' said Peter who, being young, thought things much easier than they are.

'We might at any rate go and inspect the grotto,' said Rosamund.

We went off to the corner of the garden where the grotto was. It looked very mysterious and a very suitable place for buried treasure, and even I began to think that there *might* be some there. Straggly laurel bushes cast a shadow over it, and the steps leading down to it glistened with damp.

Lionel descended the steps, unlocked the door and looked in. There were no windows, but a greenish light came through a ventilator in the roof, and when the door was wide open one could see all round the curious little place.

'I suppose it was the smugglers who brought all those shells with them,' said Rosamund, pressing close behind Lionel.

'Of course it was,' he answered. 'And now to find where the treasure is hidden.'

The floor was paved with large pebbles of different colours arranged in a pattern. In the middle was a large six-sided star made up of two interlacing triangles (which Lionel said was a magic sign) and there were smaller stars all round it.

Before very long the children had forgotten about the dangerous roof and were all inside the grotto. I smiled to myself as I watched them examining the floor, treading on each other's toes and getting in each other's light. Suddenly Rosamund screamed:

'By my halidom! One of the stars is *blue*!'

Sure enough. All the stars were made of brown pebbles except one which was made of blue pebbles.

'That's it!'

'That must be it!'

'The spades!'

'Quick!'

We tore back to the house, myself with the rest, and plunged under the wooden stairs where the garden tools were kept. This black hole was always called the conservatory by the Savages

because at home they kept their garden bric-à-
brac in an old greenhouse and they imagined that
conservatory was another name for tool shed.
Toy wheelbarrows, dolls' prams, croquet mallets
were thrown on to the heads of those at the rear
by those in front, who worked like dogs down a
rabbit hole, and soon the children were rushing
back to the grotto, each carrying some sort of
implement. I followed more slowly with nothing
in my hands.

'Do you think we ought to do it?' asked Peggy
as they bundled down the steps. 'Suppose the roof
fell in on us.'

Harry prodded the roof with a spade.

'That there roof be a-going to last another fifty
years agone,' he said in such an old, wise voice
that everyone felt reassured.

'And anyway,' said Lionel, 'we *are* allowed
to go into the grotto occasionally, and if this
isn't an occasion I should like to know what
is.' He hit the blue star with his hoe, which
being a small toy one crumpled up and the head
came off.

'We must prise up the stones one by one,' said
Rosamund, kneeling down in a puddle and
beginning to hack away with a trowel.

I had not gone inside. There wasn't any room for one thing, and for another I was getting ready to tell them that I had taken them in. I leant languidly against the door, laughing to myself to see them smash the flooring, and as I did so my hand chanced to rest on the key.

The temptation was too great. I could not resist it. Indeed, I don't think I even tried to. With all my force I slammed the door on the whole lot of them and locked it.

At once shouts and howls came from the inside.

'Here!'

'Evelyn!'

'Don't be an ass!'

'You're not funny!'

'Open it!'

'*Open* it!'

'Let us out!'

'You must!'

'Betty's frightened!'

'Open it!'

'Evelyn!'

'You beast!'

'The roof will come down and it will be all your fault.'

Their voices did not reach very far as the grotto was underground, and I walked away briskly and was soon out of earshot. I felt delighted with myself, as though I had been both good and clever, and I minced along carrying an imaginary parasol and imitating the fine ladies whom I used to see walking in Hyde Park.

Presently I met Lord Tamerlane's bath chair complete with pusher, nurse, dog, and of course Lord Tamerlane. I went up to them with my best society air, and stroked Pincher and said good afternoon very charmingly to the nurse.

'All alone!' said the nurse.

'Yes,' I said, with a little sigh. 'I find children so fatiguing after a time. Don't you?'

The nurse looked amused and said, 'Enough is as good as a feast.'

Here there came murmurs from under the rugs. Lord Tamerlane had noticed a stick lying on the lawn and he wanted it taken away. I ran to the stick, picked it up and stuffed it into a rhododendron bush. Lord Tamerlane, who had been getting quite excited, sank back relieved. However, the effort seemed to have done him good, for he fumbled under the rug and then handed me what I at first thought was half a sovereign, but it turned out to be a chocolate wrapped in gold paper and stamped to look like a coin.

'How are you feeling today?' I asked politely as I ate the chocolate.

'It's cold weather for July,' he replied in a very faint voice. I did not know whether he was trying to be funny or not.

'Perhaps it will snow,' I said. 'Then we could toboggan on tea trays. Do you like tobogganing? I mean, *did* you like tobogganing?'

'My friend Ballyshannon has very good shooting on his bog,' said Lord Tamerlane, making a stupendous effort. 'Very good, only wet ... wet ...'

His voice faded away. He was obviously exhausted.

'He doesn't often say as much as that,' said the nurse. 'He must have taken a fancy to you.'

Encouraged by this remark I walked along beside the bath chair for a bit, chatting to the nurse. Presently the bath chair was turned in the direction of the front door and the nurse said:

'Well, we've had our little walkey, and now it's time for our little snoozey.' So I said goodbye and went back over the lawn towards the grotto.

As I got nearer I grew a bit nervous as no sound came from it, and the horrid idea occurred to me that perhaps they were all dead. Someone had told me the story of the Black Hole of Calcutta, and my hand shook as I turned the key and pulled open the door. What would I see within? I hardly dared to look.

However, no one was dead, or even lying down. They were all there, standing upright, only cold, cobwebby and cross.

'I'm glad the roof didn't come in,' I said.

'Are you?' said Rosamund in a sarcastic voice, pushing past me.

Betty stopped in the doorway.

'But what about the treasure?' she asked. 'Now the door's open and we can see, aren't we going to dig for it?'

'No,' said Rosamund.

'There isn't any treasure,' I said. 'I made it all up and took you in. You were all taken in.'

'I thought all along that it was pretty fishy,' said Lionel.

'Anyone can tell lies,' said Harry. I felt this remark came badly from him but I let it pass.

'What shall we say when they ask us why we're so dirty?' said Peggy. 'We can't say we've been in the grotto because you know we're not really allowed in it at all.'

'Call it Hide and Seek,' said Rosamund.

They agreed to call it Hide and Seek.

'Oughtn't we to try to tidy up the floor?' said Harry.

The floor was rather a giveaway as they had managed to chip out a good many pebbles, but no one wanted to go back into the grotto again.

'The girls must do it,' said Lionel.

'I like that,' said Rosamund.

Of course in the end it was Rosamund and Peggy who did go back to try to make the floor look as if it had not been disturbed, but they found it impossible, as in wrenching out the pebbles the cement had been smashed up and so nothing fitted. The best they could do was to arrange a few blue pebbles in a sort of star and to throw the ones that were left over into the laurels.

'But I'm afraid they will notice the floor,' said Harry sadly. 'It doesn't look right somehow.'

'Do it better yourself,' snapped Rosamund.

Peter stepped forward.

'I know,' he said. With unusual firmness he shut the door, locked it, took out the key and threw it after the pebbles. 'That's that,' he said.

Everyone applauded him.

'You're like the friend of Charles I whose motto was "Thorough",' said Rosamund.

'Nana always does say that Peter is surprisingly thoughtful for a boy,' said Peggy.

Peter blushed, overwhelmed by these compliments from the big girls. He looked down and said modestly:

'It wasn't all me. I think it was partly the Voice of Conscience that whispered, "Peter, take that key and throw it into the laurels".'

A couple of nursery maids were seen in the distance, obviously sent to fetch us in. We were glad to see them. It was a dark afternoon and getting cold.

'I'll tell you what,' said Lionel as we moved towards the house, 'Evelyn must be tried for this. We will try her by court martial.'

'What's a court martial?' I asked with sinking heart.

'It's a military trial,' said Lionel, getting interested in his idea. 'It's what they have for spies and traitors. And at the end the prisoner is usually shot at dawn.'

'I don't want to be shot at dawn,' I said. 'Or at any other time either. Besides, you haven't got a gun.'

'We could make bows and arrows,' said Lionel dreamily. 'St Sebastian was shot with arrows.'

'I don't believe St Sebastapol was shot with arrows,' said Betty, contradictious as ever. 'He was shot with a cannonball. Grandmama told me so.'

'There's always our Red Indian tomahawks,' said Peter, tactfully changing the subject.

'And my Green Indian tomahawk,' said Betty.

I was terrified. I really believed that they were capable of killing me. Of course I might have told the grown-ups but somehow that never occurred to me. Perhaps it was because the grown-ups all seemed to belong to the Savages much more than to me. On my side there was nobody but Marguerite, and she was no good to anyone.

'Let's have it at once,' said Harry.

Fear made me unusually clever.

'No,' I said in my grandest voice. 'That wouldn't do at all. If I am to have a trial it must be a solemn one. I'm not going to have any old trial. The idea!

You've got to get everything ready and do it really properly or I shan't come to it. Tomorrow afternoon is the very earliest I could think of coming.'

'She's perfectly right,' said Rosamund. 'Charles I was kept in prison for ages before he was tried.'

'All right,' said Lionel. 'Tomorrow afternoon then. Anyway, I don't know that we could have it sooner. People would interfere if we held it in the house and I'm riding tomorrow morning, worse luck. Let's have it in the rubbish heap. The boys can be judges and the girls can be jury.'

The girls said that they wanted to be judges too, so it was arranged that some dolls should be brought out to be jury.

'What about a black cap for the judge?' asked Lionel.

Betty said there was a black cat in the kitchen but she was told to shut up. No one seemed to possess anything black, but at last Peggy remembered that there was a small black hearth-rug in her room, which she thought she could hide under her coat.

We came up to the nursery maids and Lionel said ingratiatingly to Minnie:

'Minnie, do sing us that lovely song about "They call me hanging Johnny".'

Minnie was very good-natured and began to sing it at once, little realizing the discomfort that she was causing me.

'Court martial tomorrow!' shouted the Savages as they clattered up the wooden stairs.

12. Escape

I DAWDLED behind. I felt that I had had enough of this particular house party. I wanted to go home.

As if in answer to my thoughts the baize door which led into the front part of the house swung open and Lady Tamerlane came rapidly through. She was holding a telegram.

'Oh, there you are, Everline,' she said. 'Well, I've some good news for you. Your father is so very much better that they can move him back to London. But I'm afraid that means we shall have to part with you. Your mother wants you to be there when they arrive, so you are to leave us tomorrow morning.'

At home in my London schoolroom was a picture called *The Reprieve*. A prisoner was standing against a wall. He was obviously about to be shot, but a young lady in a beautiful riding-habit had just galloped up holding out a roll of paper. Lady Tamerlane was not young and not on a horse, but she held out the telegram with a similar flourish.

For a moment the world seemed all right again, but then an awful thought struck me. Perhaps the Savages would not allow themselves to be cheated of their prey. Perhaps they would alter the time of the court martial and hold it that very night.

'Lady Tamerlane,' I said solemnly.

'What, child?'

'Will you do something for me, something very particular?'

'It all depends, child. What is it?'

'Lady Tamerlane, for a particular reason, for a *very* particular reason, I don't want the others to know that I am going away tomorrow. Would you, could you, keep it a secret?'

Lady Tamerlane looked first surprised and then amused.

'And may I ask the reason for this strange secrecy?'

'I'd rather you didn't,' I said. 'But it's nothing naughty. It's just something very particular and private.'

'Very well,' said Lady Tamerlane who was, as I hope you have noticed, always very reasonable. 'I won't mention it to the other children. And I will ask the people in the library not to mention it either. But I can't answer for everybody in the house. You must take your chance about that.'

'Thank you, Lady Tamerlane,' I said. 'You don't know what you have saved me from.'

'Can you remember to tell your *bonne* to be packed by eleven o'clock? It is very sad that you will miss the dance and she will miss the servants' ball.'

'I don't mind one scrap,' I said tactlessly, and added, 'and Marguerite will be just as glad to go as I am.'

Lady Tamerlane took no notice of this ungrateful remark and disappeared through the baize door.

By the time I got upstairs I had arranged my plans. First I got Marguerite into my bedroom and explained things to her. She could really understand English perfectly well if one talked slowly enough, and she quite got the idea that my trunk was not to be brought out till the other children had gone downstairs, and that our going away was to be kept a deadly secret.

At teatime Lionel produced a paper headed 'Court Marshal in the Rubbish Heap' which he wished to nail up on the nursery wall. The nurses, in agreement for once, prevented him, and he had to content himself with sticking it up with stamp paper in his own bedroom. I hugged my secret and was sweet and sugary to everybody.

After tea, when we were dressed and about to go downstairs, I said:

'Don't wait for me. There's something I've just remembered that I've got to say to Marguerite. You go on and I'll follow.'

The big children ran on and I was able to stop the Howliboos' nurse who was starting off with the toddlers, and I told her that I was going away in the morning and made her promise that she would not tell any of the other children. She was always friendly to me as I was nice to Tommy, and she obligingly promised at once.

Then I dashed back to the nursery where I found the two other nurses and the nursery maids relaxing, being relieved of all the children except two harmless babies. They said, 'What is it now?' rather grudgingly as I burst into the room, but they were amused by my anxiety and all promised to keep my secret.

I had thought about the other people in the house and which of them might give me away, and the dangerous ones seemed to be Mr O'Sullivan, Miss Spenser (Lady Tamerlane's maid) and Mrs Peabody. I thought I would chance the first two, but Mrs Peabody was such friends with the Glens that I felt I must warn her in some way.

The still room was a long way off; but I knew where her bedroom was, so I tore a sheet out of my diary and wrote on it: 'Dear Mrs Peabody. Will you *please* do me a great flavour. Will you *please* not tell the others that I'm going till after I've gone. Love from Evelyn.'

I underlined 'please' several times in red chalk, and then I tiptoed along the passage which led to her room. The door was ajar but there was no light in it.

I pushed the door open and heard a low growl. The gaslight from the passage showed me two eyes glaring at me from under the bed. It was Kim.

I took a step forward and Kim growled again.

'Dear Kim,' I whispered, trying to imitate Betty's voice and the way she used to speak to him, 'is he really Lord Tamerlane?'

Kim did not answer my question, but his growls grew louder. I looked round for something with which to soften his heart.

In the passage was a tray with the remains of somebody's tea on it, and that somebody had failed to eat a pink sugar cake. I fetched the pink sugar cake and threw a bit of it at Kim. He stopped growling, sniffed it, ate it and smiled at me for more. I broke the rest into pieces which I scattered underneath the bed and then, groping to the dressing table, fixed my letter to the pincushion with a hatpin.

Even when I had regained the passage I was not satisfied. How could I feel sure that Mrs Peabody (who after all was so very thick with the Glens) would be really touched by my letter? I wondered if I could bribe her with anything.

Then I remembered my beautiful and lovely glass swan which I had got in my stocking and which was the pair to hers, except that while hers had red eyes, mine had green. It was a dreadful wrench for me to part with it, but great emergencies can only be met by great sacrifices.

Marguerite had only just got out my trunk and was still putting boots in the bottom layer. I took the darling little swan off the top of my heap of

toys and also took my two last chocolate creams.
They had rather nasty fillings, which is why they
had been left to the last; but Kim, who had
finished his cake and was getting ready to growl
again, made no objection. He crunched them up
while I put the swan on top of the letter, and I got
away safely. My heart was heavy as I went
downstairs, for I had loved my swan, but I felt
that I had done the right thing.

In the library the children were jumping
round the youngest uncle and the prettiest aunt
shouting:

'Ogres! We're going to play ogres!'

'Come on, Evelyn,' said the uncle with a sort of
twinkle, 'it's ogres tonight. Tomorrow *you* shall
choose the game.'

I could not make out if he were teasing me on
purpose, and I got red and felt very awkward. I
even began to think that there really was
something a bit ogreish about him.

We played in the mysterious room called the
billiard room, in which I had never before set
foot. The glass dome was veiled in shadow and
the lights, with their thick green shades, were
hung low so that the top of the table was lit and
all the rest of the room was in gloom.

Under the table was the ogre's den. As one crawled in one came face to face with a tiger – for a moment I thought it was Kim again, come down to give me away. As a matter of fact the tiger's face was the worst part of him, as his body was quite flat with arms spread out, rather as if he had tripped up and come the most awful cropper. At the other end of the table was a leopard, smaller, but in its own way equally fierce.

When I had time to look about I found bits of other animals all over the room – heads, horns, skins, tails and even feet. The billiard balls lived in an elephant's foot and the inkpot was the hoof of a racehorse. But the most curious thing in the room was a stuffed mermaid which Lord Tamerlane, who in his youth had been a bit of a wanderer, had long ago bought in San Francisco. She was small, wrinkled and hideous, but her top half had clearly once been a person, and the tail had equally clearly once been a fish. Even Betty was silenced.

'Evelyn likes mysteries,' said Uncle Jack; 'perhaps she can explain the mermaid.'

I did wish that he would not make that sort of remark, but nobody else seemed to notice anything.

All the way round the walls of the billiard room there were seats built up on steps so that people could watch a game being played on the table. The seats had long, stuffed cushions on them like you sometimes see in churches, and Uncle Jack built these cushions into prisons for us, and though we could knock the prisons down it was very exciting. In fact, it was too exciting for Betty who soon forgot that we were only pretending, and at last could stand it no longer and broke loose and ran and ran until she reached the nursery.

I did not enjoy myself either, as I was on thorns that Uncle Jack would give me away. To make matters worse, Mr O'Sullivan came in to put coal on the fire and said casually to me (Uncle Jack had placed me on the mantelpiece):

'I hear your pa's better. And Marguerite hasn't finished teaching me French!'

I made terrible faces at him which he couldn't at all understand, but fortunately the others didn't notice anything as they were busy escaping from Lionel who had put on the tiger skin and was running amok.

I was glad when the ogre's wife said she must dress for dinner, and we went upstairs: but when we got there Rosamund and Peggy came into my bedroom with me, although I tried to say goodnight at the door. However, Marguerite had pushed my trunk behind a screen and there was only one candle alight, so they did not notice how bare my room was looking with most of my belongings packed.

'Can I look at your swan?' said Peggy suddenly.

'No, it's asleep,' I answered, pushing her out of the door. 'Goodnight, Peggy. Goodnight, Rosamund.'

'Goodnight, Evelyn. Court martial tomorrow,' said Rosamund cheerfully as they went away.

The worst was now over. As I undressed I told the pictures of the great grey stags and the little boy crossing the brook in his underclothes that this was my last night with them, and that I was jolly glad, too.

I was not out of the wood, however, and the next morning, when we were leaving Lady Tamerlane's room, her maid suddenly said goodbye to me quite loudly. I muttered something and got away, but the others had noticed.

'Why on earth did Miss Spenser say goodbye to you?' asked Rosamund afterwards.

'Perhaps she went suddenly loony,' said Harry before I could answer. 'I wouldn't be surprised if she gets sent to an asylum. Minnie's cousin's husband joined Colney Hatch and he got that fat he couldn't get into none of his clothes.'

Rosamund and Harry liked talking about lunatic asylums so much that they quite forgot Miss Spenser.

I went and played with Tommy in the nursery, and presently I heard the sound of horses being led round from the stables – clip-clop, clip-clop, and now and then a jingle. In these days children catch and harness their own ponies, but a tidy groom brought the Savages' ponies, shining and fierce, to the mounting block by the front door. These ponies were fed on oats and highly nervous. They tossed their heads, put back their ears, rolled their eyes and now and then did a few dancing steps to the side. If they saw a bit of paper they pretended to be terrified, while they never passed a motor car without shying. When they bolted, which they did frequently, there was no question of the children being able to stop them. The groom used to come thundering along behind on his big horse, cursing and swearing (or so the children said), and the whole party would go galloping along the road like a lot of John Gilpins. No wonder that when the fateful clip-clop-jingle was heard on the gravel even the daring Rosamund would sometimes be put out of action by an unaccountable pain in her middle, which would unaccountably go away again as soon as her pony was led back to the stable yard. As for Lionel and Harry they really hated riding.

With exquisite happiness I sat in the nursery window with Tommy on my knee, and watched the two boys get on to their two ponies. They were fresher than ever, I noticed, and Lionel's one pretended that he had never seen the scraper before. The groom appeared to be in his usual bad temper, and even at that distance I could feel Lionel's misery.

'Ponies vewy cwoss,' said Tommy. 'Take naughty boys away and not bwing 'em back.'

I gave him a kiss.

When the riders had disappeared down the avenue, going at that uncomfortable pace which is neither a trot nor a walk but which may turn into almost anything including a buck, I left the window and went to put on my hat and coat and boots. Just as I was ready Rosamund came into my room.

'Why are you in your best clothes? Where are you going? Why is your trunk here?'

'I am returning to London,' I said, graciously smirking, 'to my own mother and my own father. And I really must hurry. The fly will be here at any minute.'

'But you can't!' cried Rosamund; 'you mustn't! What will Lionel say! The court martial! We can't have it without you.'

'I'm afraid you must court martial someone else,' I said, smirking even more. 'You can do eena-meena for who's to be shot.'

And I sailed past her like a Duchess.

That was the end of my Christmas with the Savages. When I got back to London it was wonderful to be alone in my own schoolroom again, and the next day my mother came home and I was allowed down into the drawing room more than ever. My father seemed to me to be much the same as usual, although I was told that he was only convalescent, and for a long time afterwards he had special puddings at lunch.

And I mustn't forget to say that when Marguerite came to unpack my trunk she found something done up in a lot of tissue-paper. It turned out to be a glass swan, one with red eyes – Mrs Peabody's glass swan in fact. Round his neck was a label, 'Exchange is no robbery', and with him was a sugar nest with sugar eggs in it.

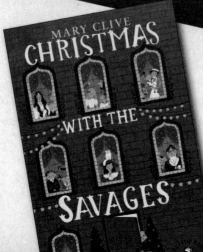

MARY CLIVE
CHRISTMAS
WITH THE
SAVAGES

ABOUT THE AUTHOR

MARY CLIVE

1907   Born Lady Mary Katharine Pakenham on 23
        August in Bryanston Square, London, fourth
        child and second of the four daughters of the 5th
        Earl of Longford and Lady Mary Child-Villiers.
        Educated mainly at home by governesses, with one
        short period at boarding school and another at a
        school of domestic economy

1915   On 21 August her father is killed in action at
        Gallipoli during the First World War

1922–6 Attends art classes at the Ruskin School of Art in
        Oxford, and later at Heatherley's School of Art
        in London

1926   Presented at court, but she does not enjoy being a
        debutante; it is much more fun running a canteen
        in Hyde Park during the General Strike

1928   *Aged twenty-one, inherits some money and leaves home, and after a brief period as a secretary resolves to become an artist. She studies at several art schools in London, Paris and Rome*

1931–2 *Goes round the world, visiting Canada, New Zealand and the Pacific*

1932   In England Now, *the first of four novels, is published under the name Hans Duffy*

1933   *Travels to India where she meets her future husband, Meysey Clive, who is one of the assistants to the Viceroy of India*

1934–5 *Works for the* London Evening Standard *newspaper, writing fashion and gossip columns as Mary Grant, and then for the* Daily Express

1938   *Publishes her autobiography,* Brought Up and Brought Out, *as Mary Pakenham*

1939   *In September the Second World War breaks out, and in December she marries Meysey Clive at a week's notice, in the Guards Chapel, in a tiara and a long white dress*

1940   *In December her son George is born*

1942   *In March her daughter Alice is born*

1943   *Her husband Meysey is killed in action during the Second World War*

1949	*Publishes* Caroline Clive, *an edition of the diary and letters of her husband's great-grandmother, a Victorian novelist and poet*
1955	Christmas with the Savages *is published*
1964	The Day of Reckoning, *about the prints and illustrations of her childhood, is published*
1966	Jack and the Doctor, *a biography of the poet John Donne is published*
1973	This Sun of York: A Biography of Edward IV *is published*
1999	*Son George dies*
2010	*Dies on 19 March, at the family home in Whitfield, Herefordshire, aged 102, leaving her daughter, four grandchildren and twelve great-grandchildren*

INTERESTING FACTS

Mary belonged to a family of clever, argumentative children. Her mother favoured the eldest brother, Edward. Like Lionel in the story, he adored putting on plays and when he grew up he ran his own theatre company.

The family lived mainly at North Aston, near Oxford, and partly in London, but in the summer they always went to Pakenham Hall in County Westmeath in Ireland, even though there was a civil war going on for much of her childhood.

WHERE DID THE STORY COME FROM?

The story is based on Mary's memories of spending Christmas when she was little with her mother's parents, the Earl and Countess of Jersey, at Middleton Park, near Bicester, which has now been demolished. Her grandmother Margaret Jersey was bossy and cultured like Lady Tamerlane. All the children are based on Mary's real brothers, sisters and cousins, except Evelyn, who is invented. Mary herself is Betty, very shy with white-blonde hair. Harry is based on her brother Frank, later Earl of Longford, who was a Labour politician and a campaigner for prison reform.

Little Tommy Howliboo is her cousin George, who became Earl of Jersey and gave his other house, Osterley Park, to the National Trust.

The First World War brought huge changes to English life. For people like Mary who could just remember life before, it was like another world, one which her children could hardly imagine. She wrote this book to help them see it.

GUESS WHO?

A *Although she was old she was brisk, and although she was not playful she sometimes gave me half-crowns.*

B *... she was a poor, frightened creature whom I treated like mud, and who hardly spoke to anybody in any language.*

C *... a fat little thing with very red cheeks and very white hair.*

D *They were quite small, pretty little things but nervous ...*

E *... had long hair that she could sit on ...*

WORDS GLORIOUS WORDS!

*Lots of **words** have several different meanings – here are a few you'll find in this Puffin book. Use a **dictionary** or look them up online to find other definitions.*

half-crown *a British coin that was used until 1967, and was worth one-eighth of a pound today*

ottoman *a piece of furniture that served as a low seat without a back or arms, and also as a box since the seat could open to become a lid*

broderie anglaise *the French term for English embroidery. It is a needlework technique that was most commonly used on women's clothing*

odious *extremely unpleasant and foul*

cruet *small containers used to store salt, pepper, oil or vinegar on a dining table*

lumber room *a room used to store big or unused objects. Similar to a storage room*

garret *an attic or small space at the top of a house that is suitable for living purposes*

puce *a dark red or purple-brown colour*

still room *a room used by the housekeeper to store preserves, cakes and liqueurs and in which to prepare tea and coffee*

John Gilpin *a leading English ballet dancer who died in 1983*

bonne *a nursemaid or housemaid who was typically French*

bull's-eyes *large and round hardboiled peppermint sweets*

QUIZ

Thinking caps on –
let's see how much
you can remember!
Answers are at
the bottom of the
opposite page.
(No peeking!)

1 **What is the name of the painting in Evelyn's room?**

a) Passing the Brook

b) Crossing the Brook

c) Crossing the Lake

d) Passing the Stream

2 **What colour are the eyes of Mrs Peabody's glass swan?**

a) *Red*

b) *Yellow*

c) *Green*

d) *Blue*

3 Where was the inkpot kept in the billiard room?

a) *The hoof of a racehorse*

b) *A tiger's head*

c) *The tusk of an elephant*

d) *An elephant's foot*

4 What does Evelyn know how to draw?

a) *Trees*

b) *Houses*

c) *Flowers*

d) *Fairies*

5 What do the children call Lionel's Secret Place?

a) *The Hut in the Woods*

b) *The Secret House*

c) *The Little Trespassing House*

d) *The Little Hidden House*

ANSWERS: 1) b 2) a 3) a 4) d 5) c

IN THIS YEAR

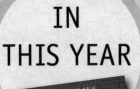

The very first edition of the Guinness Book of Records *is published and becomes a* bestseller.

African-American Rosa Parks *is arrested after refusing to give up her bus seat to a white person in Alabama, USA. Her* brave act *was a courageous step towards* racial equality.

Walt Disney releases The Lady and the Tramp.

MAKE AND DO

*A **snowman** Christmas-tree ornament!*

To celebrate an Edwardian Christmas, children like Evelyn would make their own decorations to create a festive atmosphere in their houses. Have a go at making your own snowman decoration to add a touch of Edwardian culture to your Christmas tree this year!

YOU WILL NEED:

* 1 small piece of white felt
* 3 white two-hole buttons ranging in size
* White glue
* Scissors
* Pencil
* 1 small piece of coloured felt
* 2 short pieces of ribbon

1   *Glue the buttons on to the white felt, arranging them vertically in order from smallest at the top to largest at the bottom, and so that their edges are touching. Make sure the smallest top button is positioned so that its 2 holes are horizontal, and the other two buttons have their holes vertically placed. Leave for at least 15 minutes to dry.*

2   *Use scissors to cut the white felt round the buttons, leaving a small gap between the edge of the buttons and where you are cutting.*

3   *Use a pencil to trace a small hat on to the piece of coloured felt. Then cut out the hat using scissors.*

4   *Attach the hat on to the small top button using the glue, and leave to dry.*

5   *Then wrap a piece of flat ribbon round the snowman's neck (between the top and middle button) to be its scarf.*

6   *Glue the other piece of ribbon into a looped position behind the hat. Leave to dry before you hang it on the tree.*

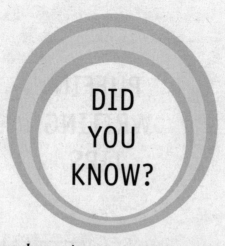

DID YOU KNOW?

Mary had **three sisters** and two of them were also writers! Pansy was a **novelist** and Violet was a **biographer**.

During her time as a **debutante**, Mary Clive spent time **modelling** for Pond's beauty products.

Mary went on **a secret trip** all by herself, cycling across France and Switzerland!

Without technology, children in the Edwardian era would use their **imagination** a lot when they played. A common playtime activity would be hosting a **tea party** for their dolls.

Hopscotch was played even in Edwardian times, and without the traffic of today it was easy to mark out the gridded numbers and **play on the street**.

PUFFIN WRITING TIPS

Make a *storyboard!* This will help you *organize* all your ideas and *plan* your story.

Keep a *diary!* Writing daily will help improve your writing skills and give you ideas for a story. Plus you'll have lots of fun reading it once a few years have passed!

Keep your *eyes open!* New ideas are everywhere around you, so pick something that interests you and *start writing!*

If you have enjoyed reading *Christmas with the Savages* you may like to read *Bogwoppit*, written by Ursula Moray Williams, in which Samantha meets a most unusual creature . . .

4. Bogwoppits

TO SEE Samantha and her Aunt Daisy Clandorris drinking a cup of tea together on the same bed, one would have imagined they had been the best of friends all their lives. Instead of which they were arguing hotly about whether they were going to live the rest of their days together or apart.

'I can't have you. You must go,' said Lady Clandorris, sipping her tea.

'I have nowhere to go to,' said Samantha stubbornly, sipping hers.

'Back to your house,' said Lady Clandorris.

'The house is sold.'

'Back to your Aunt Lily.'

'She's flying to America.'

'Go and catch up with her!'

Their voices grew louder and louder. 'I can't! She's on the plane by now,' said Samantha. '*And* her husband is. He won't have me either,' she explained.

'You'll have to work if you stay here!' snapped Lady Clandorris after a long and angry pause.

Samantha's eyes gleamed. She pictured herself as Sara Crewe and Cinderella all rolled into one.

'*I* have to work!' said Lady Clandorris, spoiling the effect, 'and I can't possibly work for both of us.'

'I will work!' said Samantha meekly.

'And live in the kitchen!' said Lady Clandorris.

'Oh yes!' said Samantha gladly.

'I live in the kitchen!' cried Lady Clandorris, 'and I cannot bear to have anyone at my heels all day long! You can only live in the kitchen when I am not living in the kitchen, and that's for certain!'

'I can stay in my bedroom, in between,' Samantha offered agreeably.

'What bedroom? I haven't got a bedroom for you!' shouted Lady Clandorris. 'I don't want you next to *my* bedroom! You probably snore!'

'Could I have an attic, or something?' Samantha asked cheerfully.

'You can have any room you please as long as you keep it tidy and stay away from me!' Lady Clandorris conceded. 'Can you cook?'

'Oh yes!' said Samantha, 'I can cook.'

'Then you can look after yourself!' said her Aunt Daisy with relief. 'I eat very little myself – mostly spinach and herbs and things out of tins.'

'Ugh!' said Samantha unguardedly. She added hastily: 'I'm afraid there is a rat in your kitchen.'

'There is not!' yelled Lady Clandorris. 'No rat at all! Never has been. You don't know what you are talking about! It is probably a bogwoppit.'

'A *what*?' exclaimed Samantha.

'You'll see soon enough!' her aunt returned, 'and the very first thing you can do for your keep is take it down to the marshes and put it back into the pool. I do it twenty times a day. I can't think how it got here. And after that,' her aunt added, 'you can make some plans for your future. I can't bear the sight of you, and shan't keep you here a moment longer than the weekend.'

Samantha did not reply. She collected both teacups and saucers, put them on to her tray, and carried them downstairs to the kitchen, leaving Lady Clandorris to get on with her dressing.

So far so good, Samantha thought. It was very much the kind of welcome she had imagined, and everything was working out according to all the stories she had ever read. Lady Clandorris was perhaps a little bit more excitable than the aunts of fiction, but no worse than Aunt Lily in a temper, and not half so noisy as the lodger, when he answered her back. She was used to being shouted at and ordered about. She had not the slightest intention of doing all the things Lady Clandorris told her to do. But she decided to begin by appearing to be obedient, and as for moving on after the weekend, she took that for one of the empty threats grownups held over children's heads, like Aunt Lily, when she said she would give her away to a home for wicked girls at the North Pole.

'They wouldn't have me!' Samantha invariably retorted.

She washed up the teacups, hung them on hooks, and looked about for some breakfast that she could eat before her aunt came downstairs. To her surprise the cupboards were well stocked. She ate two bowls of cornflakes and a slice of ham, and was pouring out a mug of milk when she heard a kitten mewing at the cellar door.

Samantha opened the door, and something hopped and shuffled into the room, something round and black and furry, with large, round, blue appealing eyes and a long furry tail. It had only two legs. These ended in wet rubbery feet with webbed toes, that seemed to join its furry legs like boots at some upper joint. Instead of forepaws it wore feathered wings, like a pair of short sleeves, and a fringe of fur or feathers fell over its eyes, giving it a fierce and furtive look. Its tail, of which it seemed supremely conscious since it never stopped swishing it to and fro, was thin like a rat's, but capable of fluffing out and stiffening like a bristle when the creature became startled or surprised.

When Samantha turned the handle of the door it had just opened its mouth (or was it a beak?) for a second mew, and she saw that the mouth was pink inside.

'Hull ... oo ... oo!' said Samantha, surprised.

The bogwoppit, if this is what it was, came flopping and shuffling into the room, leaving a damp trail of webbed footprints which Samantha instantly recognized, because she had seen them that morning on the top of the cellar stairs.

'So you're a bogwoppit!' Samantha said, rather attracted by the strange little object. 'I don't believe you are allowed to come into the kitchen, you know!'

The small creature began to hunt around the room in some anxiety, while a subdued whimpering shook its tiny frame. It searched round the table legs, bent down and frantically gobbled up some morsels of cereal Samantha had dropped. It then stood on tiptoe beside the sink, gazing upwards, and after rising and falling two or three times on the tips of its webbed feet, it rose like a small helicopter into the air, landed noisily in the porcelain sink, and began to rummage in the sink basket. Its head emerged with a frond of carrot sticking out of the side of its bill. This it chewed and spat out, looking beseechingly at Samantha.

'You're *hungry*!' she cried in astonishment, but from its perch on the sink the bogwoppit had already seen her breakfast plates on the table. Scattering the sink basket with a kick of its webbed feet, it flew into the air to land with a wallop beside the milk jug. Within seconds the milk jug was dry, and it was homing in on the box of cereals.

'Oh no you don't!' said Samantha, snatching the box away. She locked up the cereals in the cupboard and removed the milk jug.

The bogwoppit screamed with frustration, stamping round and round the table top, leaving angry, milky footmarks wherever it went, and flapping its short wings.

'Back to the cellar you go!' Samantha ordered, but when she tried to pick it up and stuff it through the door the bogwoppit bit her. Not a hard or vicious bite, but a firm, sharp, mind-your-own-business nip that made Samantha suck her fingers and eye it with indignation.

'You horrible, *horrible* little object!' she cried angrily, looking round for a duster to throw over the top of its head. 'You wait till I get hold of you! I'll take you straight back to the marshes where you belong!'

To her surprise the bogwoppit began to cry. It bowed its furry head almost as low as its webbed feet and sobbed aloud. When at last it raised its face large tears were running out of its eyes and its fur was sticky with them.

Samantha put out a hand to stroke and comfort it, risking a further bite, but the bogwoppit crept closer and closer till it was leaning against her knees. It licked her fingers with a warm, wet repentant tongue, and she felt the glow of its feathers against her palm.

'Poor!' she murmured kindly. 'Poor! Poor! Was it hungry then?'

The creature uttered a sobbing shriek of suffering. It raised its head in the air like a dog howling, making a small O of the end of its beak, and wailed aloud.

Samantha rushed for the cupboard. She filled a bowl with raisins, cereals, nuts and anything she could find. She placed the bowl on the floor, and while the bogwoppit, still choking with sobs, ate its fill, she scrubbed the dirty footmarks off the kitchen floor.

'It's rather sweet!' Samantha thought as she scrubbed. 'But I daresay Aunt Daisy has had enough of it. All the same, I'm not going to be ordered around just like that. I'll take it down to the marshes when I feel like it.' And she called out to the bogwoppit: 'Finished? Right then! Back to the cellar with you. Back!'

Opening the cellar door she pointed very firmly down the cellar stairs.

The bogwoppit began to whimper and growl. It would not go near the cellar door, though Samantha chased it all round the kitchen. Instead, it rushed at the door that led into the garden, and begged to be let out. Samantha refused to take any notice, so the creature was sick on the floor.

Furiously she turned the door handle and almost pushed the bogwoppit outside. The last she saw of it was its capering and swaggering gait as it bounced out into Lady Clandorris's herb garden.

'I hope it never comes back!' said Samantha.

Bogwoppit by Ursula Moray Williams
is available in A Puffin Book.